Lightning Falls

Praise for *Lightning Falls*:

'A glitteringly magical adventure' Sophie Anderson, author of *The House with Chicken Legs*

'Full of gorgeous magic and characters . . . beautiful' Stephanie Burgis, author of *The Dragon with a Chocolate Heart*

Praise for Amy Wilson:

'The rising star of children's fantasy' *Telegraph*

'A perfect read for those who love magic and a strong female character proving her place in the world' BookTrust on *A Girl Called Owl*

'Original and compelling . . . an unexpected tale of grief, magic and monsters' Kiran Millwood Hargrave, author of *The Girl of Ink and Stars*, on *A Far Away Magic*

'Literally spellbinding' Piers Torday, author of *The Lost Magician*, on *Snowglobe*

Books by Amy Wilson

A Girl Called Owl

A Far Away Magic

Snowglobe

Shadows of Winterspell

Owl and the Lost Boy

Lightning Falls

MACMILLAN CHILDREN'S BOOKS

Lightning Falls

AMY WILSON

Published 2021 by Macmillan Children's Books
an imprint of Pan Macmillan
The Smithson, 6 Briset Street, London EC1M 5NR
EU representative: Macmillan Publishers Ireland Ltd, 1st Floor,
The Liffey Trust Centre, 117–126 Sheriff Street Upper
Dublin 1, D01 YC43
Associated companies throughout the world
www.panmacmillan.com

ISBN: 978-1-5290-3787-6

1 3 5 7 9 8 6 4 2

A CIP catalogue record for this book is available from
the British Library.

Printed and bound by CPI Group (UK) Ltd, Croydon CR0 4YY

For Amber Caraveo

Chapter 1

The Ghost House sits upon the shore of the river, beneath a great hulking viaduct, next to a graveyard. It is built of dark, damp stone bricks that wink in the moonlight. Its windows are small, its ragged rooftops swoop down low, and lights flicker within. The edge of the river reaches out and grabs at the gardens with greedy silver fingers; the waterfall thunders and echoes throughout the valley. A battered sign swings at the entrance to the car park, metal fixings creaking with every push of the wind. *LIGHTNING FALLS*, it reads, and anybody who stumbles upon it realizes this is not the place to come for a restful night.

Of course, that doesn't matter, because nobody *does* come for a restful night. The guests of Lightning Falls come for the creaks and the squeaks, and the odd vibrating undulations of the floorboards. The rooms clatter and howl, the dining room fills with mist, and the silverware never stays still. There are dripping, echoing cellars, and dust-filled attics, and whispers all through the gardens. Many tourists used to flock to Lightning Falls in its glory days.

Now it's only a trickle, and those who do visit are either hardy ghost-hunters or here for a bargain break. We hammer and yammer about the place, and Meg does a very good shuffling whimper; and the guests enjoy our ghostly antics while drinking tea from Lord Rory's precious antique china.

Lord Rory is an acclaimed adventurer and the owner of Lightning Falls, and day to day the Ghost House is run by Mrs Peters. Neither of them is a ghost. Mrs Peters is the manager; Lightning Falls has been looked after by the people in her family for generations, ever since old Cecil.

Mrs Peters wears swishing dresses and pins her brown hair up in an endlessly unravelling bun. She divides her time between looking after the guests and looking after Lord Rory's concerns. He rarely makes an appearance, but Mrs Peters makes up for that. She watches everything we do, catching plates if they fall, pushing cups away from the edges of the lace-covered tables.

The guests love it. They love all our tricks, because that's really all they are. There's nothing dangerous about Lightning Falls – except for the cellar. Even the bravest ghost tourists do not venture down to the cellar, because there's something ancient and unknown down there that makes even *my* skin tingle.

Meg and I share a room at the top of the house where the old servants' quarters used to be, behind a huge old sign that says *PRIATE* (nobody knows what happened to the *V*). Meg has been here a long time and knows most of the ghost tricks. She can appear – or disappear – before guests at will, but mostly she's a pale wraith-like figure who pulls her hair and moans when guests are at afternoon tea. I used to go with her sometimes, but we made each other giggle, so Mrs Peters has banned us from doing a double act. It isn't *in character*, she says.

All the ghosts are related either to the ancestors who first built the house, or to those who worked here. Or they had an accident in the river that rushes and tumbles down from the waterfall that gives Lightning Falls its name. There was a railway line on top of the

3

viaduct once, but now it's just a twist of rusted metal; the last train to Upper Slaught fell off twenty-five years ago, bringing more ghosts to join our ranks and an end to the viaduct as a working rail route.

I was the latest arrival, ten years ago, and toddler-me caused a bit of a stir, by all accounts. It took them a while to work out what I was. Not quite a ghost, and not living either. A Hallowed Ghost, old Cecil says: stuck in between, and still a bit of a mystery.

Nobody has any idea where I came from, and that includes me.

The river swells now as I tromp away from the Ghost House and down through the gardens. I sit down heavily on the cold, muddy bank and stare into its depths with a sigh. The moon casts its reflection on ripples of water, and the trees on the other side whisper constantly. They have pale, cracked bark and long strands of small arrow-shaped leaves that fall like tangled hair to the river.

It's a magical place, I think. Rainbows break through the soft early mist of the mornings and, if you look in just the right way, at just the right time, there are diamonds sparkling in the deep. I love it here. When I'm feeling out of sorts, and my strangeness – my lack of known history – is bothering me, it matches my mood.

A strange, hollow sensation rushes through me as I watch the river churn, and I put my fingers to my old gold pendant.

'Valerie!'

I turn and smile as Meg comes towards me, silvery as the river. She struggles around water – most ghosts do. But not me. There's a saying that ghosts cannot cross running water. I haven't actually tried, because everybody else says it feels like having your spine ripped out, and I don't fancy that. But I can be *around* it, better than most.

'I don't know why you come down here,' Meg says, tucking herself up next to me with a shudder. She's always cold. 'It makes you moody.'

'You don't have to come out here,' I say.

'Well, I do if I want to find you,' she says.

'Maybe we should find a bell, and you can ring it.'

'And you'll come?' Her grey eyes spark.

'I might.'

I look at her for a moment. This is where she died, eighty years ago, when she was just thirteen. On the surface, if you could see us both, you'd think we were the same age. But she stopped ageing when she became a ghost, which is normal – and I didn't, which is not. She doesn't talk much about what happened on the day she died, but I know it's never that far from her thoughts. I shouldn't have her come out here for me.

'Time to go in?' I ask.

She nods. 'Mrs Peters wants us all on duty. She's fed up about the star storms, she says they've already put the *good* guests off coming, and if we're ever going to get back to full house we need to up our game.'

Meg stands and pulls me to my feet. With a groan, I follow her up the steep hill to the Ghost House. Every window flickers with light from the heavy chandeliers, and the stone on the front is darker than ever, damp with the spray of the river.

Star storms have been happening ever since I can remember. They are very beautiful – like little localized weather events, only instead of rain and clouds, stars fall instead, in clusters of bright, popping fireworks. They're not a problem if you're a ghost, but they can be off-putting for our paying human visitors. The worst was a few years ago, when an influential ghost-hunter got dazzled. He did *not* like the way he'd been caught running around the gardens screaming and terrified, and it did terrible damage to our reputation, much to Lord Rory's fury. The fact that they're getting ever more frequent doesn't help, at all.

The last one was just over a month ago. Two of our guests assumed it was a fireworks display, so they watched it, and ended up temporarily blinded by the brightness. They stayed on an extra week until it was safe for them to drive again, and Mrs Peters had to offer compensation. A ghost house is meant to be a little bit creepy, a little bit mysterious; charming, but not actually dangerous.

The cemetery looms into view as we walk up through the wild garden. Yew trees are dark shadows under the stars, and the gravestones look like giant teeth breaking through the ground. A little shudder winds up my spine and I look back to the river. From here it's a thrashing monster, rushing from the waterfall down to the ash-brown valleys, overlooked by the loops of the abandoned viaduct. The sight of the river never fails to make my chest thunder; it's awesome, and powerful, and it really doesn't care whether we like it or not. It's been here forever, always the same. Except *tonight* there's a boy sitting at the very centre of the viaduct, legs swinging, head tilted in our direction.

I blink and stare harder – there's *never* anybody on the viaduct. He's dressed all in black, like a mourner at a funeral, with glasses and longish white hair that blows away from his face in a sudden gust of wind. As I watch, a flash of silver wire breaks from his fingers and cracks through the viaduct. I stumble into Meg, who spools away like a puff of air.

'Val?'

'Sorry,' I say, when she's re-formed next to me, her mouth a wide *O* of surprise. Physical contact is tricky among ghosts; I'm quite good at it, because I'm a bit different from the others, but Meg isn't.

'Don't be using your Hallowed Ghostness on me!' she says.

'I didn't mean to! I saw a boy!'

'A boy?'

'Up there!' I point back at the viaduct.

Naturally, the boy has gone.

Meg sighs and shakes her head. I do have a bit of a reputation for making up tall tales. Mrs Peters calls them lies; my friends call them stories. I think of them as just a little extra. Facts, with a little swish of pizzazz.

But I didn't make this one up.

I stare at the place where the boy was for a long

moment, until my eyes go funny, but nothing emerges. Fog starts to curl up the loops of the viaduct, and Meg looms over me impatiently, so I turn away. I don't actually need any more drama in my life right now. Anything that sets me apart from the others more than I already am.

They always knew I was different. It was a puzzle, old Cecil says – before he worked out that I must have died at the stroke of midnight, Halloween, and that made me a Hallowed Ghost, caught between life and death. People can see me more easily than they can the other ghosts, and they can hear me. And though I was a toddler when they found me, I didn't *stay* a toddler. I've been ageing and growing, which none of the others do – they're all stuck at the ages they were when they died. And I need to eat and drink, and use the loo – Meg and I have the only en suite in the ghost quarters – and sleep. But I can float if I need to, and I can pass through walls, just like the rest of my ghost family.

Being Hallowed is not always comfortable. Sometimes it gets to me. And it gets to Meg too. She helped raise me, when I was smaller. Now I'm catching up to the age she was when she died. She says it means nothing, because in fact she's now ninety-three, but she's still a teenager really, and when I turn thirteen in a couple of weeks we will officially be the same age, in appearance, at least. Lord Rory will throw a party for my birthday – he does every year – and there will be cake, and once it's dark and all the guests are in their rooms we'll put a creepy old film on and all the ghosts will moan about how inaccurate it is, but they'll watch anyway. And I'll wonder, again, how I came to be here, and what it all really means. I'll wonder – even as I blow out candles before their smiling faces, even as Lord Rory sings louder than anyone else – who left me here as a small child.

Once we get to the house, Meg flees inside and heads to the breakfast room. She likes it in there; it's quiet and dark, and the guests are usually huddled in corners, making notes on paranormal activity.

According to the ghost rota that Mrs Peters draws up every week, which accounts for our days in neat sections of *Dawn/Morning*, *Afternoon*, *Dusk/Evening* and *Overnight*, I'm due in the ballroom now. It used to be the most glamorous room in the house, but over the generations it has faded and the carpet is threadbare, and the only thing in there that gleams is the brass on the old picture frames.

I make my way past the little wooden desk at reception, with a little nod at the (very human) receptionist, Leon. He has a pen stuck in a bun at the top of his head. He arrived two years ago as a guest looking for adventure, and never left. I guess he needed a new family too. I think he likes it here – he sticks around, so he must do – though right now he's looking a bit despairingly at Great-Aunt Flo, an ancient ancestor of Lord Rory's, who died hundreds of years ago. She is tormenting him, launching herself up into the air over and over again and floating past him, landing every time to stamp on the little brass bell. She looks at me as I pass, and winks.

Leon has his head in his hands, but straightens and puts on a bright smile when a couple come in behind me, gripping their fifty-per-cent-off promotional vouchers from the *Ghostwatcher's Express*. New guests. Leon does his best to look delighted, but I think it's hard sometimes, to be one of the few normal humans working here. Mrs Peters and Ted the chef are the only other employees who aren't ghosts. They're used to us all, but it must get draining, when you can't always see your colleagues and they don't care about things like hygiene and timescales.

'Good evening,' I hear him say, as I trail along the carpeted corridor to the ballroom. 'Excuse the bell. Welcome to Lightning Falls. As you can see, we have plenty of activity to keep you on your toes!'

The ballroom windows look out on to the grand sweep of the viaduct. The curtains here are never drawn. They're gathered on each side in great sweeps of threadbare blue velvet, tied with old ivory lace that trails to the floor. Nine silver chandeliers with dripping wax candles hang from the high ceiling, above there are several small round tables covered in ivory lace tablecloths that shift in the flickering light.

There's a bar on the right-hand side of the room, where old Cecil usually perches, up on a leather bar stool that no human has sat on for a generation. I've seen people try. They slide on, not seeing him, and then they fly off again as if electrocuted, while Cecil growls and shakes his head. He has the most amazing grey moustache that's wider than his face, and he wears an old seafaring hat that is dented at the front.

Cecil is the chief ghost, one of the original caretakers of the house, Mrs Peters' great-uncle times about a billion, and our top poltergeist. He can move just about anything, open and shut doors, *and* turn lights on and off. There's a constant shiver in the air around him, and it's cold wherever he is. He was a sea captain before he came to work here, and he says he nearly died of a shark bite; but we've never seen the scar.

'Valerie,' he says now, with a gappy smile. 'Out moongazing, were you?'

'Ah, maybe,' I say. 'I saw a boy . . .'

'Did you now?' Cecil says. 'And what did this boy have to say for himself?'

'Nothing! He was too far away. He was on the viaduct.'

Cecil goes very still.

'On the viaduct, you say?' Underneath his usual bluster, there's a sharp bite in his voice.

'Yes, which I thought was strange because nothing crosses it any more.' Not since the train came off and a whole load of ghosts showed up, including one of my favourites, Iris. 'Meg didn't believe me.'

'Ah.' His eyes brighten. 'It was your imagination.'

'Yes, my imagination does like to make up boys with white hair.'

'White hair?' asks Cecil. 'How old was this boy of yours?'

'*Boy* aged!' I say. 'And there were little flecks of lightning around him.'

'That is curious,' he says, turning away from me. 'What an imagination you have, Valerie.' He whizzes the water decanter towards us from the other end of the honey-gold bar, and grins when I catch it at the last minute. 'Have a drink, my dear. And I'll tell you all about the time I nearly got eaten by a giant squid!'

I have heard the squid story before. Approximately two hundred and thirteen times. I sit and pour myself some water, and watch his face grow animated with the rhythms of the story, and I wonder: Who *was* that boy?

Chapter 2

At dinner-time I'm in the dining hall, making the curtains swish and billow, with a little bit of whispering. It's a prime position, and not one I'm normally trusted with. Great-Aunt Flo normally does it, but she's having one of her fits of melancholy, where she keeps to the upper floors and moans and stomps about, making all the ceilings rattle, so Mrs Peters did some last-minute reshuffling with very bad grace, and here I am, twisted into the gold brocade.

I shuffle my feet against the old wooden floor, and whisper in a non-specific sort of way. Then I give a low, gibbering howl. There's a draught coming in through the patio doors, so it's not too hard to make the heavy curtains sway. Iris is floating about over the top of the tables, making the lights flicker.

There are ten tables in here, but only four are occupied: two by single ghost-hunters, who are furiously scribbling as they eat; one by a couple whose eyes dart anxiously about, as if they might be regretting their booking and would rather be somewhere nice and quiet with a hot tub; and another by a pair of older women who are watching all our tricks avidly, wild-eyed and talking excitedly.

Iris drifts up closer to the curtains and winks down at me. Sometimes her head is on backwards - a creepy reminder of the way she died in the train accident. Today, thankfully, it's pointing in the right direction – just because I'm at least part-ghost doesn't mean I don't get creeped out.

'They all look very excited,' I whisper, gesturing to the guests.

'Didn't you hear, Val?' Iris says. 'There was another star storm! Over in the cemetery. One of our ladies can see nothing but bright sparks now. Mrs Peters is just glad it didn't happen on the grounds . . .'

My chest lurches. *Bright sparks.* There were sparks all around that boy up on the viaduct. And a star storm, on the same day. Can a *person* cause a storm of bright stars out of thin air? The storms started about ten years ago apparently, around the time I arrived. Sometimes the others say that I brought them with me – but it's only a joke.

'She'll get better,' I say, rushing along the windows, running my hands over the folds of the curtains. 'They always do . . .'

'No comfort in the moment, is it?' Iris retorts, flicking up and swimming along the ceiling, red hair trailing out behind her. 'Not when there might be another star storm any night now. And all the guests will leave and the Ghost House will fall to dust, and we'll wander like lost spectres for evermore . . .'

She shakes her curls mournfully. Iris is very melodramatic. She always sees things in the worst possible light. She was twenty-five when she died, and sometimes when I look at her – and she's got her head on straight – I feel a sharp pang of sadness deep in my chest. She doesn't talk a lot about her life; not many of the ghosts do. I guess it's easier to keep busy, scaring living people who have paid for the privilege.

If I was alive, I don't think I'd pay to come to a ghost house to be spooked while I ate my dinner. I'd be off at school and running in green fields, with a little dog all of my own called Bert.

I was very small when I was found by Lord Rory, sitting on the top step of the old family crypt, and they obviously figured out that I was a Hallowed Ghost, but apart from that my background is a complete mystery. Which means that, aside from not knowing how I died, I don't remember ever really living.

Not that I'm *not* living now, exactly. Here I am, living. Even breathing. The others at Lightning Falls say that's just a mechanical function – I'm not *alive*. We know this for various demonstrable reasons. First, people can't see me, not unless I'm really trying. Second, people can walk right through me. It is not pleasant. And last, I can float. Not very high, certainly not to the ceiling, but *any* floating is *not* human.

It does make me feel strange, sometimes. Like I'm not part of the family, when in fact I'm one of the core members. All the ghosts are especially intrigued that I can eat food. Normal ghosts cannot eat. It makes Iris grumpy, so I mostly eat in the kitchen, and not in front of them.

I keep shuffling the curtains for a while, but my heart's not in it – I can't hear any of the guests' conversations, and playing with dusty old fabric isn't *that* much fun. Iris is going for it, swooshing and groaning – when she starts howling I decide it's about time for a hot chocolate, and drift off to the kitchen.

Cecil is there with Ted, the head chef. They're having a row about something called bouillabaisse, which I've no idea about, so I put the kettle on, pull up a chair and watch as things start flying through the air. It's quite a lot of fun, until I get caught on the ear by a spatula, just as I'm stirring my hot chocolate.

'Hey!' I shout, putting a hand to my throbbing ear. 'That hurt!'

They both whip around and stare at me; clearly neither of them had even noticed I was here. Then they start blaming each other. Not a word of sorry. Eventually Cecil decides to do some emergency haunting in the main foyer – one of his favourite regular guests is here and Cecil does love to flirt. That means I can sit in peace and watch Ted work while I have my hot chocolate. Ted is not a ghost, but he's very accustomed to all of us, and he likes testing recipes out on me.

'*You* try it,' he says, marching towards me with a spoon in his hand. He's very tall and thin, and regularly walks into the copper pans that hang from the ceiling. 'How dare he talk to me about flavours! It's been a hundred years since he had a working taste bud!'

I take a cautious sip and try not to grimace. Ted's a nice guy, but he does have some strange ideas when it comes to posh food. Bouillabaisse seems to be one of them. It tastes like tinned pilchards to me. Maybe it's supposed to.

'Mm, lovely,' I say, swallowing. 'What is it?'

'Fish soup!' he says. 'Can't you tell?'

'I did taste fish,' I say. 'Very nice.'

He glares at me as if I've just insulted him terribly, but fortunately Meg saves me by rushing in, making the air cold as ice. She passes through Ted, who shudders and goes back to his pot. He and Meg have a bit of a love-hate relationship; I think they enjoy winding each other up.

'Lord Rory's arrived!' she whispers. 'Let's go and see what he's brought with him this time . . .'

Lord Rory is a descendant of Henry and Isabel Falcon, the original owners of the house. He has spent years travelling the world, collecting strange things that he's very secretive about, and we never used to see him from one year to the next. He's squeamish about ghosts, which is odd for someone whose entire family is made up of ghosts, and who has essentially made a business out of them.

He's here more often now, though – and he always makes a point of being here for my birthday, which is just a few days away. Meg and I whirl away to see if we can spot him, carefully avoiding Mrs Peters, who will no doubt be in a flap; Lord Rory is very fussy about the state of the house and it's never quite to his liking, no matter how spick and span she's kept it. More than once I've overheard him telling her off for not having more *renowned* guests. He usually does his inspection with a lot of gusty sighing before shutting himself away in his private quarters in the west wing, and Meg and I hang about trying to find out where he's been on his adventure this time. His rooms are the best dressed in the whole place, and sometimes he used to let us in for tea and cake, which he ordered from Mrs Peters with a bellow through the corridors.

It's been a while since that happened last, though, and tonight we can't even get through the door to his quarters – he's reinforced it with something, and it's a no-go. Even for Meg, who prides herself on being able to walk through anything.

'What is going on?' she whispers, as we trail back down the corridor that leads to the west wing.

Great-Aunt Flo is gibbering on the landing, there's

a draught that makes the cobwebs spin against the ceiling, and I feel a bit unnerved. Meg does too – I can sense it. Something feels strange tonight. I mean, everything is always strange here, but this time it feels *different*, and not in a good way.

'Do you think he's had the door lined with iron?' Meg demands, heading helter-skelter down the stairs, blonde hair spindling out around her head, and straight through one of our regular guests, Fiona, whose faded blue eyes light up. She doesn't see us – very few of the guests actually *see* us – but she definitely felt that.

I follow after, skirting around Fiona and the elderly man who is her new companion. I don't really like going through people; it makes my heart swoop.

'Iron is *terrible* poisonous stuff for ghosts – everyone knows that,' says Meg. 'Why would he use it?'

'Because he's got secrets,' I say.

'He's always had secrets! That's part of the fun of him.'

'Maybe they're getting more serious,' I say. 'He's spent years collecting all his treasures and now he means to get rid of all the ghosts and set up as a museum.'

'You shouldn't joke,' Meg says, flinging herself up to the chandelier that hangs over the main lobby and making it swing. 'What if that's *exactly* what he's doing?'

'Of course it isn't!' I say.

'I don't like it,' she says. 'What is he doing in there, Valerie, that needs hiding with iron? I mean to find out!'

She bares her teeth as she swings, making shadows dance. The candles gutter, and the front door slams shut. A young couple who are checking in at the desk huddle close to each other, grinning as Cecil rushes right at them and straight through the door. *More* new guests – Mrs Peters will be delighted, even if Lord Rory dismisses them as riff-raff.

I say goodnight to Meg and head up to our bedroom in the attic. It's draughty as usual, and spiders skibble into the corners as I push open the trapdoor and climb in. The wooden floorboards are dark with age, and polished by years of scuffing feet. There's a large bed under the gable window in our room. I climb on to it and stare out.

The sky is clear and pricked with stars, the moon a lopsided smile over the dark rise of the viaduct. Meg will join me later. Ghosts always get an extra burst of energy in the evening. Great-Aunt Flo usually plays the piano at some point, Iris dances, and even Cecil gets a bit rowdy, telling his stories to anyone who will listen. They all love the night. They say it was made for ghosts.

For me, the night is for dreaming – strange, glittering dreams of wild rivers and towers that reach like silver spears into a star-speckled sky. But I don't want to sleep yet. I keep thinking about that boy, and the sparks that crackled around him on the viaduct.

I light the candle that's stuck into a pile of wax in an old, chipped saucer and stare at the place where he was. Of course he's not there now. I turn my gaze left, towards the cemetery. Among the giant's teeth tombstones are ancient leaning crosses and stone angels with weeping faces. Their shapes are just about discernible in the night-time gloom beneath the trees.

It's not a bad place to visit, during the day. The air is lazy, and the grass a soft green carpet. I like to take my book and read out loud, for anyone who might be listening. I've only ever seen a couple of ghosts there, and they're shy, and faded with age, so it's quiet. Which the Ghost House never is. Even now, as I take the candle and brush my teeth over the old porcelain sink, I can hear the moans of Cecil and Great-Aunt Flo down far below.

The drain gurgles, and I peer at myself in the cracked,

age-speckled oval mirror. It takes a moment, and I have to concentrate, but finally I can see myself. Dark eyes, dark hair; round, distinctly not-scary face: me, Valerie.

Cecil named me after the inscription on my pendant, which also has my date of birth engraved on it. I sigh and fog the mirror with my breath, and pull it out from under my shirt, where I keep it hidden most of the time. The gold is smooth and warm, and its face is smoky quartz. It has *Valerie* engraved on the back in ornate letters that catch the light and shine. I stare at it, wondering at the little dazzles in the quartz that seem to constantly change.

Sparks. Star storms.

Meg filters through the door. 'You spend so long peering into that thing,' she says. 'Has it told you your fortune yet?'

'Ha ha,' I say, rolling my eyes and scrambling up on to the high bed. 'It's not magic!'

The quartz shimmers in the low candlelight, and tiny gold speckles glow like stars. It's just the same as ever, I tell myself; but I know that's not true. Somehow, today – ever since I saw that boy – things have *shifted*.

I grip the warming metal in my fingers. It feels solid and comforting. I'm not always so good at holding on to things: I drop cups, if I'm not concentrating, and sometimes my hand goes straight through things like banisters and tables. For some reason, though, the pendant is always solid.

Cecil says that because it belongs to me, it's bonded to me in some special way, and I should be careful never to lose it. I'm not sure, but I do know that Meg's never been able to get a grip on it, and she's pretty good at holding things, at least for long enough to throw them at people.

'What are you thinking?' she asks.

She settles down next to me and I hide the shiver that creeps over my skin. She's always cold, and I wish my body wouldn't react in the way it does – I'd hate for her to notice.

'It feels like things changed today. I just don't know what.'

'Maybe you grew an inch,' she says. 'In time for your birthday!'

I snort. 'I do know it doesn't work like that.'

'*Now* you know,' she says with a wicked grin. She stares at the pendant. 'Do you ever wonder where it came from?'

'Where *I* came from, you mean,' I say. 'Not that it

really matters – we're all a bit of a mystery here, aren't we?' I bunch the quilt on to my lap, tucking my hands into its soft folds.

'But I know *my* history. I remember my family.' Meg is silent for a moment, her gaze distant as though she sees her mother and father, and the older sisters who used to pull her hair and sneak her sweets. She blinks them away. 'And you don't. All you have is this pendant.'

'And Cecil's stories.'

'But we all know Cecil can't be trusted!'

I frown at her. We've had variations on this conversation before but never quite like this. I feel like Meg's pulling at something, and I don't want her to. Especially not today, when everything already feels strange.

'You don't think he's been honest about how I came to be here?'

'Valerie, you know what he's like. What do I think? I think it's a mystery. You're a mystery. Now that you're nearly thirteen, I thought you might like to start . . . investigating.' She draws out the word slowly, and it sounds silvery on her tongue.

'Meg!'

'It's fine if you don't want to,' she says. 'But when you're ready, I'm ready too. We can work it out together.'

'Work what out, exactly?'

'What being a Hallowed Ghost really means! Where you came from, who your parents are.'

Every word hits like a hammer, right where all my doubts are sitting. I don't like it.

'*This* is my family, Meg. You're my family. It doesn't matter what came before!'

There is a small silence.

'It does, you know,' she says at last. 'It does matter where you came from, even if you're happy with where you are now.'

I sigh. I do want to know where I come from. But I also want to be happy here, with the people who brought me up, and the two things don't necessarily go together. Lightning Falls is all I know, and I've been happy with that for a long time.

I curl into the cold sheets, and tuck my hands under the pillow, and Meg curls up next to me, ready for our evening read of Agatha Christie. But tonight my eyes won't stay open. I dream, and my dreams are strange, magical adventures through strange, magical streets, and though she doesn't know it, Meg is with me the whole time. My strange, ghost sister, flitting like an ice fairy by my side.

Chapter 3

Meg isn't with me when I wake. She often isn't – she gets restless, and she doesn't really need to sleep, like I do. I shake off my dreams and the lingering warmth of streets paved in smooth, coppery gold, and head down for breakfast.

I find Ted in the kitchen, listening to jazz while he whizzes around clattering pans. The sun filters through old wood shutters, half open. I stay out of his way, hooking my feet through the rungs of the bar stool and blinking away the rainbow shards of light that always follow those most vivid nights.

When I was small, Ted had a team of sous-chefs, dishwashers and even a waiter. He loved to bustle around, watching them with a hawk eye and shouting when they got things wrong. But his staff were let go as the Ghost House got quieter, and now it's all on him, so he moves like a tornado.

After a while, he slides a bowl down the counter towards me. It's porridge with brown sugar and winter berries, and a lick of cream from the blue-and-white-striped jug.

'Thank you,' I say, stirring it all together to cool it down.

He flashes me a quick grin before ringing a brass bell and barking out that table five is ready. Mrs Peters bustles in, says good morning with a ruffle of my hair and sweeps out again with the tray, and Iris filters through the door to smell the coffee – even though she can't drink it, she still appreciates the aroma. It's all very ordinary.

All very ordinary, except it's not. The strangeness of yesterday is still with me – the bright stars in my pendant, Meg's ever-growing insistence on solving the mystery that brought me here – and the boy on the bridge . . .

I eat my porridge as quick as I can, and, thanking Ted, I hurry out of the kitchen and escape outside into the quiet, and the cold fog of an autumn morning. The roar of the waterfall as it smashes down the rocks is like the roar inside me. I walk towards the river as though drawn by a magnet, down the rough old stone steps at the bottom of the garden. My pendant snags in my hair, and I pull it free – and that's when I see him. The strange boy from the viaduct, walking, head down, straight towards me. Tiny black and silver sparks make the air around him seethe, so bright that my vision swims and he seems to vanish entirely.

I stop. He raises his head and notices me. Dark eyes flash, then he rushes past me up the steps, straight up to the Ghost House. I run after him, but by the time I've made it through the old revolving doors – they're very hard to walk *through* when they're still rotating – the lobby is empty. Black-and-white floor tiles shine under the already-lit chandeliers. I scan the stairs and the doorways, but there's no sign of the mystery boy.

'Morning, Valerie,' says Leon. 'You came through there in a rush! What's wrong?'

'I thought I saw someone come in,' I say.

'Not for the last few minutes. We did have a check-in earlier, quite an interesting one – a lady who saw one of the star storms on her way here. Mrs Peters took her straight off to her room – she could hardly see the hands in front of her face!'

32

'Did she come with someone?' I ask.

'Oh! Yes, she was with her mother.'

'Not a boy?'

'No, Valerie. No boy – just the one star-struck, with accompanying mother.' He frowns. 'Unless I missed somebody. Though that's not likely.'

I sigh. 'No. Never mind.'

Leon nods, taking a sip from a bone-china cup, and goes back to examining the massive bookings ledger. We tried using a computer a couple of years ago, but most technology doesn't work well around ghosts, and it ended up being mayhem.

I look around. Where did the boy go? He definitely came in, and it is strange that Leon didn't see him. Then again, even *I* could hardly see this particular boy.

He must be here somewhere.

The Ghost House is a vast place to try and search. There's the ground floor, with the reception, dining room, kitchen, library, ballroom, breakfast/sitting room and Mrs Peters' office; then four floors of bedrooms, along winding corridors; and the attic, which has several further bedrooms and a couple of old, clanking bathrooms. And finally the cellar, where

Meg and I never go; we got locked in by mistake once with whatever lives down there, and though nothing bad happened, it definitely didn't feel good. We were very glad when Great-Aunt Flo unlocked the door and hauled us out.

I start out on the ground floor (as good a place as any), treading endless reams of red carpet covered with little white diamonds. The walls are papered and there are lanterns lighting the way, flickering whenever a ghost is nearby – which is always.

'Morning, Val,' says Meg, floating around a corner just as I reach the first floor.

'I saw that boy again!' I say. 'The one from the viaduct yesterday. He's in the Ghost House!'

'Where?'

'I don't know. I saw him come in, and then I lost him.'

'Is he staying here? A few new guests arrived . . . one of them star-struck!'

'Leon said.' I think back to the boy, running up the steps in a haze of sparks. 'I don't think he's a guest though – Leon said he hadn't seen him. He had little flecks of lightning around him, Meg, I swear it – and he just charged in! What if *he's* causing the star storms?'

Meg's eyes light up. 'Oo! Now that would be exciting – imagine if we find him, and he *is* responsible, and we can put a stop to it all! You look on the upper floors and I'll search downstairs. We can present him to Mrs Peters at our morning meeting!'

'Meg . . .'

But she's gone, rushing down the passageway towards the dining room, sweeping clean though an older couple, who stop and shiver, grinning to each other.

I shake my head. I don't want to find the boy only to drag him before the whole family. He didn't look exactly dangerous. More like lost, and lonely. Meg needs to stop reading so many Agatha Christie stories. To her, everything is a mystery to be solved right now – including me.

Chapter 4

Meg and I didn't find the boy that morning. Or the next. We hunted for him between all our usual duties but there was no sign, and I'm starting to wonder if he *is* still somewhere in the Ghost House, hiding, or if I really did imagine the whole thing.

I huff now, and crack my knuckles. Day three, and Meg is definitely starting to go with option number two. One of my rota tasks is to go around the guests' bedrooms with a trolley, topping up packets of tea and biscuits, since as a Hallowed Ghost I can handle those things better than the other ghosts, and we had to let go of most of the human staff. I normally do a fairly cursory (bad) job of it, but today I'm determined to find him. So I take the opportunity to search every inch of every bedroom, from the creaking four-posters with the bay windows that look out to the gleaming river – to the smaller, darker rooms at the back, where Mrs Peters puts the bargain-hunters.

Only a handful are occupied, but I take my time and investigate every corner, even poking through the adjoining bathrooms, where my reflection in mottled mirrors stares back at me, hollow-eyed and worried.

'For goodness sake,' I tell myself at one point, catching an accidental glance of myself as I audit the soaps. Brow furrowed, hunch-shouldered, half in shadows – I look haunted. I'm in a slightly damp single bedroom, rarely used because it's right on the corner where the waterfall roars loudest. 'It's OK. Everything is OK.'

The plughole in the old, cracked bath gurgles, and the little window blows open. A swirl of bitter wind rushes around the room; the waterfall thunders and fills the air with a fine spray of water. I shiver.

'Meg?' I whisper.

But it doesn't feel like Meg. Meg gets too excited when she's trying to be scary, and gives herself away. It's not Cecil, or Iris, and it's certainly not Mrs Peters. It isn't even Great-Aunt Flo. It smells like musty old books.

Careful, Valerie, comes a whisper through the wind. There's a flicker in the mirror, the shape of a girl. *He's getting restless. He'll take it if you don't hold tight!*

'Who?' I demand, turning to find the source of the voice. 'Who will take what?'

Only silence. The wind eases.

I have to stand in the bath to close the window. I gaze out. The waterfall is at full pelt after a barrage of splattering heavy rain last night, its surface alive with white foam. I lean out and breathe in the mist of Lightning Falls, tasting it on my tongue. Sparks swim like bright fishes through the tumult. The clouds part overhead and for an instant I feel a pull towards the water, a physical thing that makes me stretch too far out of the window, my ribs grazing the ledge.

A trace of laughter far down below breaks the spell, and I pull myself back, closing the window with a snap.

'Do you mean the boy?' I say into the ether, climbing out of the bath. 'Is *he* the one getting restless? What's he got to be restless about? What does he want to take?' But there is no reply; whatever it was that whispered to me has gone again, and left nothing but more mystery.

Outside in the corridor, Mrs Peters catches me and hustles me downstairs for the mid-morning mass-cacophony in the lounge. It's customary for us all to pile in together and screech and ransack the place – carefully, of course, so as not to break any china – while the guests drink tea and eat little sugar biscuits. Their eyes are wide as they watch spoons (Cecil's) floating through the air, and shadows (mine and Meg's) flickering on the wall beside the fireplace. Iris is steaming up the window and drawing kittens with her fingertip, and Great-Aunt Flo is up by the ceiling as usual, humming an old lullaby.

I tuck myself in by the old dresser and look around at the guests. No boy, naturally, but there is a young woman, about Iris's age, who I haven't noticed before. She's sitting on a small sofa by one of the windows, staring out into the fog with a dreamy look on her face. She must be the one who was star-struck. An older woman next to her – her mother, I suppose – reads from a book about Gothic architecture.

I linger a little closer, and the younger woman whips around from the window, staring straight at me.

'Frankie?' says the older woman, looking up from her book.

'Such beautiful lights,' Frankie says, her gaze passing through me. 'Really, Mother, they're just magical.' She reaches for a biscuit.

'So magical you can't see the plate in front of your face!' Her mother snorts, guiding Frankie's hand.

'Oh plates.' Frankie sighs. 'I've seen a thousand plates.'

'But lights that blind must be stared at.' Her mother shakes her head. 'What made you turn just now?'

'For a moment, I thought I saw a brighter light,' Frankie says. She turns her head back to the window. 'It's gone now.'

I frown, moving slowly away from them. What did she see when she looked at me? A light? I look down at the pendant in my fingers. The flecks of quartz are glowing. It's just normal, I tell myself. Just like it's always been. But the star storms did start about the time they found me, in the cemetery. And now the boy is here, with sparks a little like these escaping – and the storms are getting worse.

Where is that boy?

There's only one place I haven't checked yet. The cellar.

Of anywhere in the house, the cellar is the only place I ever feel truly haunted. Shivers run down my neck the moment the door slams behind me; whispers flash about the darkness as I grip the wobbling banister and head down creaking steps.

Mrs Peters comes down here every once in a while to light the fire and stop the whole place from rotting, and always comes up even more wild-haired than usual. Great-Aunt Flo is the only one who is comfortable here. She doesn't come down often herself, but she says it's cosy; it reminds her of other times, when the house was young.

It doesn't feel cosy to me. It's a vast space: there's an old chaise longue against the wall by the fire, and a threadbare rug in the middle of the bare stone floor. At some point the bricks have been whitewashed, and now the paint has faded and chipped; swathes of white flakes fall to the floor as I run my fingers along the wall.

There's something old and strange here – older and stranger than any of the ghosts. We all know it, even if it's never been seen. When Meg and I were down here before, there was a definite feeling of being watched, which made my skin prickle. The place has an eerie vibe: smoke filters through the air vents, silver chains snake from hoops set into the floor, ready to trip and trap, and the whispers never stop. I stare into the darkness and there's a violent shudder in the air – a boom that isn't sound but the presence of that same *something*. I wrap my cardigan more tightly around my shoulders, ignore the shiver running down my spine, and hurry towards the yawning old fireplace. I put on kindling from the bucket and prod at the embers with a poker. An orange glow builds, throwing more shadows on to the ceiling.

'Hello?' I whisper. 'Was it you, before, telling me to be careful? I didn't understand your warning. Are you here?'

'Who are you?' comes a harsh voice behind me.

I spin, the poker raised in my hand. It's the boy from the viaduct, just inches away. He moves back, frowning, and all the hairs on the back of my neck stand up.

'What are you going to do with that?' he demands, nodding at the poker. Tiny wires of blue light lick at the floor around his feet.

'Nothing!' I manage, lowering it to my side. 'What are you doing here?'

'I was investigating,' he says. He looks around at the room. 'This is a very strange place.'

That puts my back up. 'Only if you don't know it well,' I say.

He moves closer and I lift the poker a little. He's

taller than me, but only by an inch or so, and he's bony. His clothes are close-fitting, and though they're black they've got tiny flecks in them, brightly coloured shards of blue and green that flash in the firelight, like scales. There's a thundery shiver in the air around him that makes my chest tighten, and behind bright, wire-rimmed glasses his eyes sparkle like the river that rumbles now through the old stone walls.

'What are you investigating?' I demand.

'Magical things were stolen,' he says, wincing as silver veins of light flick across his face. 'And this house reeks of magic. I thought it was a good place to start looking, but I got stuck down here; the door wouldn't open.' He steps closer, brow furrowed. 'What is that around your neck?'

'M-my pendant,' I stammer, wrapping my fingers around it. 'I don't know about magical things.' I lift the poker a little higher, to remind him that I have the upper hand, though it trembles in my grip. I wish Meg was here. My palms are sweaty, my heart beating too fast.

'But it's an Anchor,' he says. 'I can tell that much, at least. So I was right – they *are* here! Where are all the others?'

'The others?'

'Don't play games with me – the other Anchors! Stolen belongings, full of magic from Orbis! They don't belong on this side of the river.' He frowns, takes a step closer, looks me carefully up and down. 'And neither do you. Why are you here?'

'That's what I wanted to ask you!' I say. 'You're the one with explaining to do. You're in my *home*, uninvited!'

He watches me for a long moment, as though he's puzzling something out. 'This is not your home,' he says eventually. 'I don't know what kind of place this is, but I know you don't belong here.'

You don't belong here.

Words I've danced away from my whole life. How dare he speak them so casually, as though he knows anything at all?

'YOU don't belong here!' I shout, the words burning through the storm in my chest.

He flinches, eyes wide with shock. The room darkens around us. The *something* in the cellar grumbles through the fireplace. The boy looks frightened, and if he's really been down here for two days, it's no surprise. I try to calm myself. He obviously needs help.

'This is a bad place,' he says. 'I came down here and then . . . I couldn't leave. I felt something, tugging . . .' He looks around, shivering. 'Never felt anything like it before. It's eased now, maybe because you're here.'

'It won't hurt you. You just need to concentrate on getting out. I can come with you . . .'

'No thanks,' he says, turning his back. 'I can concentrate just fine on my own.'

The floor sparks beneath his feet as he walks away. He fades up the stairs and disappears through the door.

He's a ghost.

I should have realized. I feel a pang of regret. I should have been kinder to him, more understanding. It's sad when a new ghost doesn't realize that they've left their old life behind. It happens sometimes here, especially when people are young. They just don't believe it.

He's just a deluded ghost. And yet . . .

You don't belong here.

I've always been different. Not family in the blood sense, not a ghost in the ghost sense. Most days that's fine, and I appreciate that I can eat a crumpet, but there are days it's lonely, and I wonder who my parents are – who gave me my dark hair and brown eyes. Whether I laugh like my mother or walk like my father. Meg was right. It *does* matter where one comes from. People like to know these things, ghost or not.

I sigh and give the fire a savage poke. Ash drifts from the grate on to the floor, and a deep sigh echoes mine.

Truth will out, comes a whisper behind me, making me jump. I spin, poker still in hand, but there's nothing here – nothing visible, anyway.

'What do you mean?' I whisper, shivering. 'What *truth*?'

But there's only silence, and then the door at the top of the stairs bangs open and Great-Aunt Flo comes trailing down the cellar steps, her lace skirts rustling. She has faded gold hair that is tied into a long plait that snakes down her back, and soft wrinkles around her brown eyes. 'There you are, Val! You look as if you've seen a ghost!' She trills with laughter.

'There are just too many weird things going on, Aunt Flo.' I sit on the old chaise longue, ignoring the puff of dust and creaking springs. 'A new ghost boy was just here. He said there were stolen magical things in this house. And Lord Rory's put iron in his door, my pendant is sparking like the river, the star storms are getting worse – and I'm being followed by somebody *else* who wants to warn me about something but won't show themselves!'

'That is a lot,' Great-Aunt Flo says, looming closer. 'Perhaps you should stop flinging yourself around the house in a panic and sit down with a good book. Books often have answers.'

'To everything I just said?'

'You might be surprised,' she says, looking back over her shoulder. 'This is the time to be curious, Valerie.'

'That's what Meg says. She wants to investigate.'

'Good for Meg! You don't?'

I am quiet for a minute. 'He said I didn't belong here.'

'This boy of yours? Did you believe him?' Great-Aunt Flo frowns, and levitates a couple of inches. Her brown boots are faded, the laces trail like a child's.

'No.'

'Good,' says Great-Aunt Flo. 'Find the right book, and start at the beginning.'

I stare at her. 'What is this about?'

She rolls her eyes. 'I'm trying to help you, Valerie. But there's only so much I can *say*.' She lowers her voice. 'You'll need the ladder – it's on the top shelf to the right of the fireplace, far left. Slim volume. I'd get it for you, but I've always been a butterfingers and it's a very old book. It might fall to pieces if I drop it. Come on.'

I get off the dusty chaise longue and follow her up the cellar steps to the ground floor, where Cecil's mid-afternoon lobby storm is in full swing – he makes all the lights flicker, and booms about the place like an old ship. Great-Aunt Flo vanishes to join him and I head to the library.

There are lots of books about ghosts here, aimed at our guests. Great big old things that look like they're made of wood, with gold writing on the spine and titles like *Spook Sisters* and *The Tale of the Headless Horse and His Man*. Then there are more modern paperbacks, tragic love stories, supernatural encyclopaedias, some classics, and a lot of mysteries (Mrs Peters loves them, and Meg often reads them over her shoulder).

Top shelf to the right of the fireplace, far left. Slim volume. I move the ladder from its resting place by the door and swish it along its runners past the fireplace. The polished wood is cool as I start to climb, and as I get higher the smell of the books gets older and mustier.

I sneeze, and a load of dust spirals out from the shelves. I recognize these books – old, handwritten leather-covered journals. Mrs Peters told me they're hundreds of years old, some of them dating right back to the building of the house. I did glance at one a few years ago, but it seemed to be full of shopping lists, the words tight and curly, really hard to read. They give me a creepy feeling.

The very furthest to the left has a thin spine, covered in faded green leather. I edge it out. It looks like some kind of journal. The name *Ada Falcon* is stamped into the centre along with the year: 1727. Truly ancient.

I tuck the book under my arm and clamber down the ladder. Then I curl into my favourite blue chair, next to the fireplace, and let the warmth of the room comfort me as I run my fingers over the soft leather, letting the pages fall open.

Ada

The waterfall thunders! It sounds quite as though it will wash us away, and I have said as much to Papa, but he says the house was built of the very strongest stuff, and that it will withstand the constant hurl of water.

Papa lived here as a child, and says he always meant to return, when the time was right. That time has come, with Mother's passing. It is grey and drab, but it is our ancestral home and so Papa says we must make the very best of it.

He remembers the glory days, when it was filled with light and music – which is hard to picture, now. Everything is faded and dusty. It's not that which I mind though, or the waterfall – it is the strangeness of the whole place.

I am sure that Lightning Falls is haunted, and not only the house – there is something peculiar about the river it is named after. On the most cloudy days there are rainbows in the water, and when the sun is shining it looks as though the whole riverbed is made of gold.

I have not dared to speak of it to Papa, or to

my old nursemaid Jemima; I am sure they would just think me ill. I have whispered it over little Florence's cot. She looks up at me with her wide blue eyes as if she truly is listening, and even quite understanding it all!

I am careful to make sure Roger isn't within hearing; he does hate it when I make up stories. He says I do it to try to be like our mother. That isn't true, but it fills me with shame every time he says it. How could I possibly be anything like her? Mother was like the sunshine, and the roaring sea, and the low, quiet song of the moon, all together. I am just a small, plain girl trying to keep the house from sinking into perpetual mourning.

Roger hates what he calls my 'flights of fancy' – he says it is unseemly behaviour. When Papa is in his study – which is most of the time – he does lord it about the place. He is older than me and remembers coming here as a small child, when our grandparents were still alive. He despairs at the way it has been left to rot while we were in the city.

He moves things, orders the servants about, and gets most particular about routine and order. The fire must be laid and ready at all times; the silverware must gleam; supper must be fit for a king; every candle lit (he has always hated the dark, and this house does seem to collect it in the corners); and the portraits on the wall be straight to a hair's breadth.

He misses Mother's tendency to perfection, and the parties she hosted that filled our old townhouse with society people, and he misses Mother herself most of all, though he will not say as much. His sadness all comes out as spikes. His voice has recently broken, and sometimes when he raises it – usually at me or Cecil, the old caretaker we inherited with the place – it rings out in a peacock shrill that I might laugh at, if the words weren't so mean. Cecil quite hates him already, and glowers about the grounds muttering old sailor curses under his breath. I have collected quite a few exciting new profanities, though I shall not share them here!

Fortunately for both Cecil and me, Roger is away at school most of the time, and as soon as he is gone we all breathe easier. I am glad to be away from the city, and the new nanny is very sweet with Florence. Papa's mood does grow brighter, day by day, and though the house is prone to darkness, and strange noises, it is grand and beautiful.

Papa has allowed me to help in the choosing of new furniture and curtains; new things arrive every day, and bring much-needed excitement, if only for a while. The wallpaper is flocked, and the carpets are deep, so it does feel cosy. The grounds are lovely to wander in, and so are the gardens; even the misty little cemetery over the wall has a charm about it, so I mean to ignore the strangeness and be happy – for Papa's sake, if nothing else.

Chapter 5

I don't read any further. I stare at the words until they blur.

The river sparkling with rainbows even on a grey day. Cecil, and *little Florence*. Was that Great-Aunt Flo? Is that why she wanted me to read Ada's journal so badly? Books often have the answers, she told me. I squeeze myself deeper into the armchair, tucking the book under my thigh. That boy pulled a thread and Great-Aunt Flo grasped it, and now my pendant is thrumming between my fingers. I remember the hunger in the boy's eyes as he noticed it. When he told me I didn't belong. I know that if I stare down at it right now, it will be sparkling just like that river water, so I don't look. Instead, I wonder.

What if Cecil did make up the bit about me being

a Hallowed Ghost? There are no books here about Hallowed Ghosts; I've never found a reference to another one, and we all know that Cecil does like a tall tale. The shark that bit him while he was wrestling a giant eel. The pirate ship that he boarded before it was destroyed by an octopus eight metres long. When I was little I could listen to him for hours. His eyes would light up and his big hands would spread wide as he talked. I knew all the punchlines, all the really good bits. I'd sit by the fire with Small, the ghost deerhound, at my side, and we'd all roar like lions when he got to the bit where he was marooned in a land far away.

Cecil made his way here from all his adventures, he says, looking for a little quiet. He was here long before Lightning Falls was a Ghost House; when it was an old manor house, with stables and golden carp in the pond that's now just full of weeds. And according to this journal, he was here when Ada Falcon and her sister Florence were just girls, missing their mother – and he was a rogue, teaching them his old sailor swear words. Making up stories, no doubt.

A born storyteller.

And one of the stories he told me was my own.

He says Lord Rory found me in the cemetery. It

was freezing cold, and the Ghost House was full of light and laughter – in those days it was busy, full of paying guests. Rory had been out for one of his evening constitutionals; he'd always loved the night-time for walking, Cecil said. When he came back in he was soaked through, holding a small child – me.

I don't remember any of what came before that, no matter how hard I try. I suppose about two years old is very young. But you'd think there would be *something*. Everybody else here knows how they died, how they came to be here. All I know is that Lord Rory found me.

'He was charmed by you,' Cecil would say, as he tucked me into bed, lighting the lamp. 'He tried not to show it, but I could see the gleam in his eye when he carried you in, fast asleep. Good job, really. You've been eating him out of house and home ever since – and he never was the kind to do anything he didn't want to do.'

'When did you all know I was a Hallowed Ghost?' I would ask Cecil.

'That first night. You woke, and screamed the house down, until Ted came out and gave you a slice of bread. We thought he was mad, but he knew. Picked you up and took you to the kitchen, fashioned you a high chair out of a bar stool and an old wooden crate, and that was that. Our special girl. Our little Hallowed Ghost.'

'Meg says I'm a mystery,' I told him once.

'All the world is a mystery,' he had said.

'But she says she's never heard of another Hallowed Ghost.'

'Meg does not know everything,' Cecil said. '*I* have heard of them. Far and wide I have travelled, and there are many things out there that defy explanation. There is an explanation for you. And besides, you are family. That's the only thing that really matters.'

I think now about the strangeness that Ada must have felt. The generations of ghosts who lurk in Lightning Falls. What if the reason we're all here is not family, but magic?

This house reeks of magic. That's what the boy said, in the cellar.

There is one person who would be able to tell me more about the night I was found, and that's Lord Rory. But he has locked himself away, to do goodness knows what. It *could* be magic, for all I know. The idea of Lord Rory being all wizardy in the west wing, in a tall hat and star-spangled cloak, makes me smile.

I take the book with me up to the attic. I don't look out at the river; I just pull the curtains closed with a shiver, climbing into bed and tucking the journal under my pillow before reaching for Agatha Christie. Stolen objects, magic, Anchors. It's all too much to think about now. Logic is what is needed. Tomorrow I will find that boy, and it will go better. I will make sense of everything, tomorrow.

Chapter 6

Our weekly Monday morning staff meetings are always a bit of a farce. Mrs Peters is determined to keep holding them. I think she read about them in a magazine once. She says that we are a business, after all, and meetings are part of the territory. But nobody takes them seriously – and today is no exception.

Great-Aunt Flo is blowing at the fire in Mrs Peters' office until it's like a furnace, Meg is practising being invisible by the window, and then Ted comes in with a mixing bowl to show how busy he is. Once he came in with a great big wad of dough and started kneading it on the desk, sending a cloud of flour over everything. Mrs Peters watched and the corners of her mouth twitched, but today she is looking especially stern. She ignores the bowl in Ted's hand and stands in front of the window, a faint golden halo around her as the low autumn sun filters through, her arms folded, mouth pressed thin while she waits for us to settle.

Eventually, everybody does.

'First of all,' she says, looking around us, 'Lord Rory will be permanently in residence for the next few weeks. He is busy with a new project and requires absolute privacy. The west wing is therefore strictly out of bounds.'

Cecil rolls his eyes. He and Lord Rory do not get along.

'That means you must all stick to your posts,' Mrs Peters goes on. 'Either haunting the guests, or in the common room . . . or in your own quarters.'

'Or outside,' I say. I don't like being told where I can and cannot go.

'Nobody is denying you your moon-eyed excursions to the cemetery, Valerie,' Mrs Peters says, making me blush. 'We are merely reiterating what you should already know. Lord Rory is of course, as ever, grateful to all of you for making the Ghost House everything it is today.'

I catch Great-Aunt Flo's eye. We all know Lord Rory is deeply disappointed that the most we can muster is chaos and a steady trickle of ghost-hunters.

'Secondly!' Mrs Peters says, raising her voice. 'We have a new guest who has been recently touched by the star storms. We will be taking extra care of her, of course, and we will not all be staring at her and asking a million questions!' She glares at Meg, who shifts beside me.

'I only stopped for a polite chat,' she mutters. 'There must be some reason that the star storms are getting more frequent . . .' She gives me a glittering look. 'I thought I'd investigate. She's called Frankie, and she's studying botany at university. I do love botany, you know.'

'Do you even know what botany is, Meg?' asks Iris, perching on the windowsill.

'Flowers!' squawks Meg. 'Of course! Anyway, Frankie says she can see things *better* now, in a way. Things she'd never noticed before . . . For instance, she could see me, clear as day! She says she has a friend who is very interested to hear about her visit here – he's a bona fide ghost whisperer. She says *he* won't be afraid of a little thing like a star storm—'

'Our guests are not here to be investigated,' interrupts Mrs Peters severely. 'They are here for hauntings. Not for interrogation!'

Meg lifts her chin. 'Talking of interrogation, Valerie has seen a strange boy, covered in sparks.'

Everyone stares at me. I widen my mouth in a smile and try to look innocent.

'Is this the boy you spoke to me about the other day?' Cecil asks.

'Yes.' My mind whirrs, and I decide not to say anything about our encounter in the cellar. Great-Aunt Flo winks at me, as if to say my secret is safe with her, and I hope it is – I haven't even told Meg yet, and she'd be furious that I'd kept her in the dark.

'But he is real?' demands Mrs Peters.

'Yes! Of course he's real.'

'You *did* have that imaginary friend,' she says with narrowed eyes. 'Lesley, wasn't it?'

Everyone starts nodding.

'That was years ago!' I protest.

'Right. Well, should anybody come across a strange boy covered in sparks, bring him to me immediately. Other than that, no bothering the guests!' Mrs Peters says, with another pointed look at Meg.

'Frankie was happy to talk to me,' says Meg, hovering just over the arm of the chair I'm sitting in. 'She was nice. She's never been in this part of the country before.

They parked the car and went for a little wander, and then, as she put it, "the sky burst into diamonds"! She told me it was "oh ever so pretty" and that she can *still* see the trails in front of her eyes!'

'And precious little else, I'd imagine,' says Great-Aunt Flo. 'Those star storms are a portent, I'm telling you. Never used to happen – now they're bursting out all over the place. I saw one out of the window just last night, like golden freckles in the sky.'

'You're lucky they don't affect *your* eyes then,' says Iris. 'Why are they happening so often, I wonder . . .'

'Magic,' cackles Great-Aunt Flo, with a sly little wink at me.

'Thirdly!' Mrs Peters chimes, as if we're all just a collection of irritating noises in her head. 'Somebody has been playing silly beggars in the pantry and Ted is not happy about it. He has a very precise way of organizing his items; blowing in there and messing them up is not funny.'

Ted glares at us all, nodding. 'The flour in particular is not funny. Floury footsteps. Flour everywhere.'

'Maybe it was a guest, looking for something to eat,' I say, looking at Great-Aunt Flo. She's folded herself into the darkest corner of the room, and her brown eyes gleam. She looks like a flour-treading mischief-maker to me.

'The guests do not need to search my pantry for food!' Ted protests. 'They are well fed, constantly, and to a high creative standard. They do not need to go truffling about disturbing the flour.'

'Quite,' says Mrs Peters, brushing down the front of her dress as if she's somehow managed to get covered in flour herself. Her own gaze lands on Meg (again). '*Whoever* is doing it, just stop it. Any other business?'

'What's Lord Rory done to his door?' Meg bursts out beside me.

Everybody turns to stare at her.

'What do you mean, Meg?' says Mrs Peters.

'I went to check in on him – you know how he has a soft spot for me,' she says. 'And,' she goes on, ignoring all the sceptical looks, 'the door repelled me.'

Cecil frowns. '*Repelled* you? As in . . .'

There's a collective indrawn breath. Meg nods.

'As in *iron*,' she says. 'And I know he's very important and we're not to bother him – but iron is still banned here, isn't it? What's he doing, anyway, that he needs to hide away?'

'Iron is not allowed in this house at all,' Cecil

blusters, standing. 'We will not have it, Mrs Peters. Does he mean to drive us all out?'

'I'm sure there's a simple explanation,' starts Mrs Peters – then the door swings open and a tall, spindly man sweeps in, his silver-grey hair swept up in a great peak atop his head, his customary pink-tinted sunglasses perched on his nose.

Lord Rory.

The room turns a couple of degrees colder as all the ghosts shrink away from him. He *never* comes to these meetings. There was a rumour once that he'd had an iron filling in his teeth so that none of us could get close to him, but it isn't true, Mrs Peters says, because we're 'his family'. *Creepy or not*, she says, *he chooses to be here, and that's because he loves us.*

She can never quite look you in the eye when she says that bit.

'Family!' he says now, with a broad smile. 'I couldn't help but overhear some of your conversation. And I think . . .' He looks from Mrs Peters to the rest of us. 'I think that a little reminder of your, ah, circumstances might be useful. This is a Ghost House, and for as long as it operates to *some* degree you are welcome here. But first and foremost Lightning Falls is my home, and in the eyes of the law, it is *only* my home, and *only* belongs to me. Therefore, if there is some small corner of it that is out of bounds to even my nearest and dearest –' his gaze lingers on me for an instant – 'then that needs to be respected.'

Everyone is completely silent. Great-Aunt Flo is making faces from the ceiling, Meg is pouting like a fish, Cecil has retreated to a patch of gloom in the corner away from the window, and even Mrs Peters looks affronted, her hair standing on end.

'Furthermore,' he says, his glance sliding across Meg and Iris, and settling with relief on the solid form of Mrs Peters, 'let me assure you that our future is my topmost concern. Everything I do is to secure the safe future of Lightning Falls and all those who *live* here. The house is in constant need of repair and attention, especially if we mean to attract the very best of society. The day of the ghost tourist is over. We must bring this place out of the shadows and into the light, for all our guests!'

'Must we?' pipes Great-Aunt Flo. 'I always think the best sorts of people like a little bit of darkness, myself.'

'Fortunately, it is not *your*self who is in charge,' snaps Lord Rory. 'Luckily for all of us, I have a plan. For that, I need privacy.'

'I'm sure we are happy to leave you in peace,' says Mrs Peters. 'Though I still don't understand quite why *iron* is necessary,' she adds, sounding uncharacteristically tentative. 'And I don't know about the day of the ghost tourist being over. People will always be intrigued by ghosts, and we have the very best!'

'You don't need to understand any of it,' says Lord Rory. 'You are here because I allow it, and if you don't behave yourselves, I'll sell the whole place to developers and they'll knock it down.'

'Lord Rory!' says Mrs Peters, drawing herself up.

'Of course it won't happen,' he says smoothly. 'We love this ghastly old pile, in one way or another. You must simply trust me. Quite apart from anything else, some things – some very special things, just around the corner – need a little secrecy!' He looks at me again, and his eyes gleam behind his rose-tinted glasses. Then he turns and walks out.

'He meant your birthday, Valerie!' Meg says. 'He's keeping us out because he's planning something spectacular!'

'I don't know,' I manage, flushing as everyone stares at me. 'It's not that big of a deal!'

'Thirteen is special – he's said that before, hasn't he?'

'I can't see how a birthday surprise justifies iron,' grumbles Great-Aunt Flo. 'Even if it is a special one.'

We are all silent for long moment.

'Well,' says Ted eventually, with a sigh. He picks up the bowl. 'Lunch won't make itself.'

Everyone trails out after him.

'I wonder what he *is* planning!' Meg whispers when we are outside, and when I turn to look at her she's just about gleaming with excitement. 'I am going to be keeping a very close eye on Lord Rory!'

I shake my head. I've always thought Lord Rory was kind, behind all the glowering. I love his glittery glasses, and that he always has a smile for me. When I was smaller, he'd bring sweets every time he returned to Lightning Falls, and he's always been home for my birthdays, but I'm not sure all that really accounts for the iron in the door.

'Maybe we should leave him to it,' I say. 'If it's a surprise . . .'

'Oh poo,' Meg says. 'He's hiding more than a birthday cake – I want to know what!'

She flits off to the breakfast room to read the newspapers over guests' shoulders, and Great-Aunt Flo sails past me to the lounge, clearly having been listening.

Trouble everywhere. I make a list in my mind:

Lord Rory, acting very strange.
The boy with sparks and his lost objects.
Ada, and rainbows in the river.
My pendant, the ghost in the cellar, star storms . . .

It's a lot, and none of it makes sense. I turn back to the library, and Ada's story.

Ada

I do not believe in ghosts. They are the sign of a weak mind; macabre tales told to frighten children. Florence giggles when the curtains billow without the wind, and I don't believe that she sees a spirit there. It's just a ravel of a breeze.

The river, however. That is a different story! There is a mystery there, deep within. I have taken up painting with watercolours so that I may spend hours on the riverbank, studying the shift of light, the spark of something like magic that is growing ever harder to ignore.

I must write of it here, because I cannot speak of it. Papa is a fair man, and kind, but he is not one for superstition and legend; I think it would suit him if all the world were just the same as he. I am glad it is not. I love him, but it gladdens my heart to feel that there is more to the world than straight lines and common sense.

Jemima would like to know what on earth I was thinking, 'out in the cold without a shawl'. She bundled me up in a blanket so tight, it has taken me quite a minute to unwind my arms for writing! I have not told her either, though I know she suspects I am up to something. And she, too, has noticed the strange activity in the house: flickering candles and curtains that shift when there's no breeze; creaking floorboards where nobody treads. It is hard to light fires even when the wood is dry. She has told the nanny never to leave Florence unattended, not even for a moment, though she does not say why.

I was relieved when she said it, I have to admit. Florence is still so small and fragile.

I do miss Mother. She was a quick wit, and the most wonderful piano player. Any house is quiet without her, and the piano is still now; she was not a patient teacher, my fingers fumbled where hers flew, and I cannot even go near it. Nor can Papa, and Roger won't go into the music room at all when he is here, which is less and less often; he cannot stand the haphazard ways we have fallen into here; he bemoans the slow pace of life, and the chill in the air, and seems to prefer the company of his room-mates. I cannot say I am sorry.

Perhaps Florence will be the one to play the piano, some day.

There is something on the other side of the river.

I have become quite obsessed with the whole mystery. I spend hours down here by the river, pretending to sketch or paint, watching the water rush by, while Nanny coos over Florence under the shade of the old oak tree in the garden.

And last Monday, just after breakfast, I saw something.

It was running just below the viaduct. A fine strand of golden wire. It curves, like a second bridge over the water, its other end disappearing into the mist thrown up by the waterfall. Some days, it is hardly there at all. Other days, it is a ribbon that bends and twists into the distance. And once or twice, as I've been looking, it is a rainbow, bright and vivid, catching the light and dazzling me.

There is magic here, I think. For certain.

And I am already discovering that magic is not safe. The first time I saw the rainbow I looked too long in wonder, and my eyes did sting for hours afterwards. I had to lie in my darkened bedroom for a day and a night before the feeling passed. Dear Florence must not come down here – she is too tiny now, but as she grows she will surely adventure as

I have, and I begin to feel that I shall spend my life catching her and saving her from dangers.

Such is the life of a big sister, I suppose.

Chapter 7

Night falls with a crash and a bang at Lightning Falls. I've always found the chaos soothing; you're truly never alone here. But tonight, sleep won't come. Meg is with Iris, howling through the old pipes, scraps of old songs and lullabies that make me think of Ada and her little Florence, who is now an old-lady ghost with faded hair and a knack for lounging on ceilings.

Frustrated, I unwind myself from my sheets and creep downstairs, out into the bluster of night, and the pale light of the stars. The old gate from the Ghost House grounds to the cemetery always creaks when it opens, and tonight I don't want anyone to hear, so I clamber over the wall beside it instead, tying a knot in my nightie and scrambling up, my bare feet finding familiar ledges.

The moon emerges from the clouds just as I land in the long grass of the cemetery. The grey tombstones rise before me, row after row, broken by the monuments of richer folk: angels with wings spread; massive crypts with boarded-up doors.

I say hello to the familiar names: Mary, who died aged sixty-nine in 1923; Gregory Thomas, a curate who died during the First World War; and Lionel, who is remembered by his name alone. It isn't just old people here. Normally I make a special point of going around the younger ones, touching the headstones nobody visits any more, saying their names out loud – but not tonight. Tonight is for silence, and thinking.

I head for the crypt at the centre of the cemetery. It rises ahead of me, old grey stone pitted and marked with the bright green fur of lichen. I run my fingers over its smooth surface, imagining myself here as a toddler. Trying to picture the person who left me. There was a single moment in which that happened. When someone turned their back and abandoned me. I close my eyes and visualize a small child standing just where I'm standing now, perhaps on the same kind of blustery near-winter night. The yew trees rustling, stars flicking in and out of sight behind the clouds, cold air wrapping around warm skin. A grown-up, cloaked and hooded, taking one last look back, before slipping into the darkness. I screw my eyes tight in concentration, but all I can make out is the smudged outline of dark against dark.

Nothing else.

I open my eyes and stumble into the crypt, where Henry and Isabel Falcon – the original owners of Lightning Falls and ancestors of Lord Rory and Ada – were interred. Maybe they saw what happened; maybe they watched over me until Rory arrived, only resting when they knew I was safe.

I know it's fanciful. I like it anyway. I imagine them dressed in stiff silk, wearing old powdered wigs, sitting on top of the tomb where both their names are inscribed, waiting with me until Lord Rory stumbled upon me.

'It didn't work out so badly.' I sigh, running my fingers over their names before resting up against the tomb.

'Didn't it?' comes a familiar dry voice.

I start. It's the boy. The new ghost, sitting across from me on the floor of the crypt, his eyes dark behind his glasses. He's wearing a thin, dark cloak, the hood now pulled up over his white hair, a messenger bag flopped onto the ground beside him.

'What are you doing out here?' I ask. It's no wonder he looks so thin and miserable if this is where he's staying; it's creepy out here, even for a ghost.

'I could ask you the same,' he says.

'I live here! Well, in the Ghost House.'

'I had to get out of there,' he says. 'There was too much noise.'

'It is bustling, especially if you're not used to it,' I say, sitting down across from him. The cold stone bites into my skin, and I notice he's shivering. So he's not a normal ghost. I stare at him. Might he be another Hallowed Ghost? A flare of excitement rushes through me at the thought that there might be another like me.

'When did you die?' I ask gently. 'Do you remember?'

'I'm not dead!' he says, scrambling to his feet. 'What kind of question is that? What kind place *is* this?'

'It's a Ghost House,' I say. 'You know, a haunted house, where people come and stay to be . . . haunted.'

'And you *live* here?'

'Well, yes. With the other ghosts. It wouldn't be much of a Ghost House without us!'

'You aren't a ghost,' he says, shaking his head. 'Why do you think you're a *ghost*?'

I take a deep breath and remind myself that he's new to this.

'I *know* I'm a ghost,' I say. 'I've been a ghost ever since I can remember.'

He doesn't take his eyes off me. 'I can see your breath steaming out when you talk,' he says eventually. 'Aren't ghosts supposed to be dead and cold?'

'I'm a *Hallowed* Ghost,' I say. 'I died on Halloween, so I do still breathe and grow, and eat things. Maybe you're like that too. You're probably hungry – you've been here for days. Do you remember when you died? I know it's complicated, but if you died on Halloween, you could be a Hallowed Ghost like me.'

He turns to the wall and puts his head against it. I wait, patiently.

'I finally track this place down,' he mutters to himself, 'after all this time . . . and now I'm stuck here, and it's a crazy place where girls think they're ghosts.' He groans. 'It's impossible. I can't bear to go back into that house, and everything I need is in there.'

'I'll help,' I say. 'If you come in with me, I can introduce you to everybody, and it'll start to feel like home. You'll see – everybody's lovely, really. What's your name?'

'Joe,' he says. He turns round to face me again. 'What's yours?'

'Valerie,' I say.

'How long have you been here, being a ghost?' he says.

I get the impression he's humouring me, but I answer anyway. 'Ten years, nearly,' I say.

'And how did you get here? I mean, presumably you *died* here somehow?'

'I was found in the cemetery.'

He looks around at the crypt. 'Here? So close to the river?'

'Well, yes. Just on the steps. Lord Rory found me and took me into the house. They brought me up.'

'What kind of ghost needs bringing up?' Joe shakes his head. 'They convinced you for all this time that you're a special kind of ghost who grows up and breathes?'

I swallow. Why is this so hard? Because he's new, and scared, I remind myself, and he needs help.

'I think the others might be able to explain it to you better,' I say. 'Why don't you come in and stay for a bit? At least you wouldn't be alone . . .' And he could meet Meg, and she could help me figure all of this out.

'I don't want to stay in a Ghost House.' His dark eyes

glitter, and tiny blue sparks wind up the wall behind him. There's something so brittle about him, like a false note in a melody, slightly too sharp and making the whole thing sound wrong. 'Because I'm not a ghost. Neither are you.'

'Then how do you fade out of sight?' I say, trying to be reasonable. 'How do you walk through walls?'

'I suppose it must be the magic,' he says. 'It works differently over here.'

I sigh. 'What is this magic, then?'

'I'm from Orbis,' he says. 'It's another world, over the river – over the bridge. And there's magic there.' He tilts his head, appraising me. 'The kind of magic that might make a small child seem like a Hallowed Ghost.'

A pang goes through me – it's as if he's looking right at that small child, the one I've never been able to remember properly. And he looks so sad about it.

I push the thoughts away. 'You made fun of me for thinking I'm a ghost, and now you're telling me you're from a magical land on the other side of the viaduct?' My heart lurches, even as I challenge him. *Over the river*, where Ada saw such wonder. The river, that calls to me and sparkles under the sun.

'Not the viaduct exactly – there's a bridge built of Orbis magic running parallel. Maybe you haven't noticed it,' he says. 'It hasn't been used for years, and it's glitchy. It took all my magic to cross it. But yes, I'm from a magical land. A long time ago some things were stolen from us – very important things.' That sad look again, as he stares at me. 'I could feel the pull of the magic, so I followed it – but that cursed house is a maze. I don't want to go back in, and I can't get back on the bridge either.'

'Why not?'

'I used up my magic getting here,' he says. 'Then I got trapped down in the dark, which didn't help.'

'What *are* these stolen things you're looking for?'

'I told you before, back in the cellar! The Anchors,' he says, sounding impatient now. 'They're the magical devices that store our magic. Like the one you're wearing.'

I put my fingers to my pendant, then draw them away.

'It isn't magic,' I say.

'Isn't it? I think you're full of magic. You're from Orbis too. These *ghosts* found you in the cemetery and didn't know what to make of you. They had probably never heard of Orbis, or the magic over the other side of the river, so they came up with a story – where you're like them, but special.'

I stare at him, and all the tiny wiry sparks that wiggle over his skin, and the breath spirals out of me. For a moment I can't breathe in. My heart thunders, and my skin is all prickles. *Special girl.* That is what Cecil would call me. Or Rory, when he lights the candles on my birthday cake. I'm just like them, only *special*.

'That isn't true,' I whisper eventually. 'I'm trying to help you and I don't even know why. You're causing problems here. Like the star storms . . .'

'Star storms?'

'Sparks – that hurt people's eyes! They've been getting worse, and then you appeared.' I eye him. 'You're all static and dangerous.'

He blinks. 'You mean *this*?' He gestures to the blue sparks that swarm over him. 'That's my magic, building up. I haven't started any star storms.'

'Oh?' I say. 'Well, something's been making them worse.'

'What you're talking about sounds like magic *escaping*,' he says with a frown. 'From magical objects . . . like the Anchors! I *knew* they must be in the house –

I can feel the magic from here. That's *why* I'm here! If we can find them, I can take them back with me, and that might stop your storms.'

He sounds so desperate that I almost want to stop fighting and believe everything he's saying. But I can't. This is *my* crypt, in *my* cemetery, in *my* world. *The* world. Surely there isn't a whole other world out there.

'I don't know if I can help you,' I tell him. 'I need to go.' I edge towards the crypt's doorway.

'No, don't go – wait!'

'I'll come back!' I manage, as I flee down the steps.

Rain starts to fall as I rush through the old gravestones, and Lightning Falls looms ahead of me, its windows bright and warm against the dark stone. Someone's taking out the bins, and I can see Mrs Peters in her office, reading the paper. Iris appears at the dining-room window, head on backwards, singing. Normal things that happen every day, even in a Ghost House.

I keep my eyes forward as I jump back over the wall. My feet skid on the grass as I land, but I catch myself before I fall and I don't stop to think, I just keep running over the grass and the gravel, until I'm safely back inside.

Chapter 8

Ada's diary is under my pillow, but I don't look at it. I just sit on the bed, and stare out of the window, and listen vaguely to the noises of the Ghost House all about me. It's the early hours of the morning now, but there is never silence.

The gutters spew water out on to the old, lichened patio, and the river is a roaring mass as it tumbles down past the viaduct. On the other side rises the dark mass of the woods, and past them is Upper Slaught, where the trains used to come in. There is no magic there. I've never been, but it's where Mrs Peters directs people to gift shops and a country pub for lunch. They come back with postcards of tiny stone cottages and a church that's hundreds of years old.

It isn't called Orbis. Because there's no such place.

Joe must have died in a storm; perhaps that would explain the sparks. He's confused.

Which makes two of us.

I put my fingers to my pendant, and the old gold is warm to the touch. I know every angle of it, every edge, every facet. Joe called it an Anchor, and that feels so right, because it is my anchor. It is the thing that connects me with the child I was, when Lord Rory found me. That's not magic, though. That's just having a very old, beloved thing.

'Why are you hiding up here?' Meg asks, appearing through the door. She swishes up closer to me. 'You look strange, Valerie. What's wrong?'

'I found the boy,' I say.

'You did! Where was he?'

'He's in the old crypt.'

She grimaces. 'He's going to haunt the crypt? Hardly original – and not very clever, really. He'll just be on his own all the time – nobody ever goes there. Except you!'

'He says he's not a ghost.' I blink back sudden tears, mostly of frustration, but Meg sees everything. She always has.

'You've been having adventures without me!' she says, sitting next to me on the bed, with a rush of cold air that makes me shiver. 'Tell me everything.'

So I go back to the beginning – finding Joe in the cellar, reading Ada's journal, all the talk of magic, and the river, and Joe's insistence that I'm not a Hallowed Ghost, and neither is he.

'Did you put him straight?' Meg interrupts at that. 'How else could he float through doors like you said he did?'

'That's what I was trying to *tell* him!' I say. 'I think he's delusional. He had this story about magical objects called Anchors. He thinks they're in the house. He said he's from a place called Orbis, over the bridge – and he says I am too.' I look at her, hoping she's about to say it's all nonsense, but she's wide-eyed, caught in the story of it all. 'I think he *must* be a Hallowed Ghost like me, because he was shivering, but I couldn't get him to believe me . . .'

'So he's just out there now, shivering?'

I shrug. 'He wouldn't come into the house. He said it's too noisy.'

'Well he'll have to get used to that, won't he?' says Meg. 'Surely better in here than out there.'

'I don't know. He was sparking again. It might not be safe for the guests, Meg.'

'But if we don't believe in the magic and the Orbis-world thing, then there's nothing for us to be afraid of, is there?' She gives me a long, level look. 'Did you make him up, Valerie?'

'No!' I scowl at her. 'I'm not five, Meg – and this is too important!'

She nods. 'So let's go back together. I'd like to see this boy for myself.'

'It's raining,' I say, peering out of the window. 'Let's go in the morning.'

'But the best adventures are at night-time! Anyway, you can't stop me.' She curls away from me, and starts for the door. 'I'm going. Come with me! We'll take some cheese – he's probably hungry, if he's a Hallowed Ghost.'

I sigh and haul myself up, following her across the landing to the stairs. 'You – you don't think he's right, do you, Meg?'

'About what?'

'That I'm not a ghost. And we're both from this magic place called Orbis, over the bridge.'

'Over the bridge is Upper Slaught,' Meg says firmly. 'But maybe he *does* know something about you, Valerie. Something about where you both come from.'

I hide the shiver that runs through me, and we cling to the shadows as we rush downstairs, past all the mayhem. I creep into the kitchen and manage to get a bottle of water, some cheese and a piece of cake from the fridge while Ted's arguing with Cecil about coffee beans. As I go out I run into Great-Aunt Flo and she winks at me.

'Best food is nicked at midnight,' she whispers.

'Are *you* the pantry thief, Flo?' I ask.

'Right now, it looks like it's you!' She giggles, before filtering through the kitchen door.

I don't hang about to find out what sort of chaos she's about to cause. Meg is waiting by the front door and we head out together, a blanket and one of Mrs Peters' best feather pillows under my arm.

'So much trouble if we get caught,' says Meg breathlessly, as we flee towards the gate and the cemetery. 'We should do this more often, Valerie! What an adventure.'

She's buoyed up by the thrill of it all, but it doesn't last long. The river isn't kind to her; its rushing so hard that by the time we get to the crypt steps, she's ragged with old fear. I stick close to her, though it makes me colder, and press my hand against hers.

'We can go back,' I say. 'It might be easier in the morning, Meg.'

'It's OK,' she says, as we head up the steps of the crypt. 'Just –' water trickles from her hairline and floods her footsteps – 'memories aren't always easy. Anyway, we're here now. Where's the ghost boy? Ghost boy!' she howls. 'Are you here?'

A dark heap in the corner of the crypt stirs, and Joe raises his head.

I take a step towards him. 'Joe . . . I brought some food . . .'

'And a sister,' says Meg.

Joe looks up. His eyes are dark, and the pupils spark with tiny blue lines.

'Whew,' says Meg, rushing over to him and sitting opposite, nose to nose. 'That *is* strange. How do you do that?'

Joe winces, shuffling back.

'Meg, meet Joe,' I say. 'Joe, this is my sister, Meg.' I sit along the wall a bit from him, and thrust the water at him, laying the pillow between us and placing the food in its paper bag on top. 'We thought you might be hungry.'

'Do ghosts get hungry?' he asks, after drinking

heavily from the water bottle.

'Well, yes and no,' says Meg. '*Technically* no, but also yes, because I see your cake there and I want some. And then there are Hallowed Ghosts like Valerie, who can eat. So are you going to eat it? Because that would make you a Hallowed Ghost, like she is.'

'Or a normal person,' he says.

'Normal people don't spark,' I say.

'They do in Orbis,' he says. 'If their magic isn't under control, that is.'

'So your magic is out of control.' Meg shakes her head. 'That *is* a problem.'

'Yes it is,' he says.

He opens the paper bag and pulls out the cake, eating hungrily. Meg and I watch him in silence. I never have met anyone like him before. Of course my experience is limited to the Ghost House, but there have been plenty of guests over the years, and none of them made the air thunder like he does.

'Thank you,' he says when he's finished eating.

'We think you should come into the house,' Meg says. 'You feel the cold, don't you? Like Valerie does.'

'Valerie is also from Orbis,' he says. 'The more I think about it, the more sense it makes.'

'You think Valerie is a magical girl from another world? Like you?' Meg shakes her head. 'You have a funny idea of what makes sense. How did she get here then? Someone just brought her over your bridge and left her in the cemetery? Who would do *that*?'

'I don't have all the answers,' Joe says. 'I wasn't expecting all this. I thought I'd come over, get the Anchors that were stolen and head straight back. I didn't expect to find strange girls and *Ghost* Houses.'

'Why would these Anchors be in our house, then?' I ask. 'Who do you think took them?'

'We know who took them,' he says. 'Thieves from Orbis, selling our most valuable things over here. They were caught coming back over the bridge, and arrested. But we never found out quite what happened. The bridge became unstable after that, crossing it was banned, and the Anchors were never found.'

'When did all this happen?' demands Meg.

'Ten years ago.' Joe glances at me. 'About the same time you arrived here, it sounds like.'

'And they never found the Anchors,' I whisper. 'Was there a . . . a missing child, too?'

'There was,' he says in a low voice.

There's a long silence. The crypt is dark, and water

91

trickles down the stone into the corners.

'So your theory,' says Meg, 'is that somebody stole these precious things from your world – and took Valerie too – and brought them all here, and left them, and then went *back* and got themselves arrested and locked up? Why would they do that?'

'Nobody could work that part out,' Joe says, rubbing his face and pulling the pillow on to his lap. He looks exhausted. 'Their Anchors were missing too. They said they didn't remember what had happened. Without their Anchors, their magic was uncontrollable – they were barely able to remember their own names. And the Anchors they'd taken were all gone. The thieves were put in the tower, and eventually all those people whose Anchors were stolen had to be locked in there. Without their Anchors their magic was out of control too, and they were a danger to Orbis. There are wards on the tower that disrupt magic, so that it can't do any harm.'

Meg looks thoughtful. 'And nobody ever worked out what really happened?' She glances at me.

'No,' says Joe. 'But at this point it doesn't really matter. I don't care *why* they did it, or how, I just want to get the Anchors back. My pa's was stolen. He's been locked up in that tower for years.'

'So that's why you're here – to find his Anchor, and save him,' I say.

'That does sound nice and heroic.' Meg nods. 'A good story.'

'It's not a *story*!' Joe bursts out. 'Not one I'd choose, anyway.'

'Well –' she brushes it away – 'are you causing the star storms?'

'No, that's the stolen Anchors,' he says. 'They're leaking magic. You see Valerie's pendant?'

They both turn and look at me. I hold out the pendant.

'That's her Anchor,' said Joe. 'It's not making sparks because it's with her. It takes her magic, and stores it, and as long as she has it she's fine. As long as I have mine, I'm fine, though mine's always been a bit glitchy . . .'

'That's why you're sparking.'

'And because I used a lot of magic to get over the bridge to be a hero,' he says tiredly. 'The sparking will all settle down when I've built my magic up again. Look . . .' He takes a pair of tiny binoculars out from under his shirt. The wooden case gleams, and copper eyepieces sparkle in the light. 'Here it is. Ma reckons there might be a bit missing and that's why I've always

93

struggled a bit with magic. I think that missing piece is here somewhere, and *that's* what drew me over the bridge.'

'Where does your family think you are now?' I ask.

'Ma doesn't know where I am. I hadn't planned on being here for very long,' he says, huddling deeper into his cloak.

'You didn't tell her? She'll be worried!'

'Yes, she will be,' he sighs. 'It wasn't exactly intentional, I thought I'd be here and back within a day. Things . . . got complicated.'

'Everything is complicated,' says Meg. 'You'll need our help to find these Anchors, I suppose. We can hold an investigation. What are we looking for, exactly?'

'All sorts of things. Pocket watches, bangles, charms – you'll know them if you find them.' He looks at me. *'You'll* feel the magic, since you're from Orbis.'

'I'm a Hallowed Ghost,' I say, backing into the wall. 'Not your lost child. Not magic.'

'Fine,' he says. 'You can think what you like – but carry out your investigation first.'

Meg glances at me, raising an eyebrow.

'OK, Valerie?'

'OK. Let's go.'

I storm out of the crypt, glad to be away from Joe. The air is biting cold, the river a monstrous churn that matches the feeling deep in my belly.

'It'll be all right,' says Meg, her eyes firmly fixed on me, her face turned from the river.

I look down at my pendant. The gold stars within flicker, sending tiny vibrations through my fingers. I always thought I wanted to know more about where I came from, but now I'm deeply regretting that. I love my family. They're not just ghosts, there to spook and entertain the guests. They're my brothers and sisters and aunts and uncles. We spend our time bickering and teasing each other, and we love each other. Does that change if I'm not a ghost? If magic is real, and I'm something else entirely?

'Stop panicking,' says Meg, as if reading my mind. 'We don't know anything yet. We're going to try and help this boy find these Anchors so that we can send him home again over his *fractured bridge*. There might not be any such thing . . .'

She peers back at the river and I follow her gaze. I can't see a parallel bridge, or much at all, just the massive arches of the viaduct, and the mist that rolls off the waterfall.

'He's probably a Hallowed Ghost, like you,' she says. 'We'll just humour him, for now.'

Somehow, I feel like she's humouring *me*.

'That diary I found,' I say. 'It belonged to Ada Falcon – descendant of Henry and Isabel – and she lived at Lightning Falls in 1727, when Great-Aunt Flo was just a baby. They were sisters. *She* talked about strange shimmering in the river. And now Joe says there's definitely magic in there, and magic hiding in the house . . . What if Lord Rory is hiding *magic* up there in his rooms, and he's known all along?'

'Then it's about time we found out,' Meg says.

And she skips up the steps, into the porch. Flickering lanterns make a golden glow of the mist that comes off the river, and the flagstone steps are soft with lichen. The massive door swings open as we approach, and Iris swishes up to us mid-air, beckoning us in with a smile, singing '*Where have you gone to, my lovelies?*' and floating off to join Great-Aunt Flo at the piano in the drawing room before we can answer.

'Come on,' says Meg, drawing me inside. 'This is our chance – it looks like Frankie has cornered Lord Rory about being star-struck. She is wonderful.'

Chapter 9

I follow Meg through the Ghost House, and she moves through the air as if she were part of it. I am heavier, clumsier, but when she reaches back her hand and I take it, my own feet lift and we are floating. Sisters, adventuring together through the chaos.

We pass a couple all dressed up for dinner as we head for the west wing. They're making for the ballroom, where I can hear Iris tinkling already; she likes to play with the tall crystal wine glasses, especially since it makes Mrs Peters wince. I blow lightly on the candles in the sconces so that they bubble and flicker and send jagged shadows of us up the walls. The man gives a little skip, hooting with nerves as we brush up and through them. When we turn back, the woman is lit up with the most enormous grin. She can't see us, but her eyes are trained right on the air around us.

They're the ones who make me curious. The ones who feel us here and are happy about it. Cecil says it's because we're evidence that there are strange and wonderful things in the world, even if people can't normally see them.

My feet hit the ground as we head around the next corner, nearing Lord Rory's rooms. Something is different here, something that makes my chest ache. I stop, staring through nothing. The corridor is just the same as ever. Moonlight falls in a shaft through a narrow window, filling the air with a thousand tiny flecks of dust. Ancestors of the house stare at us impassively from their heavy antique frames, dark oil strokes glittering.

Meg hovers beside me. 'Val, what is it?'

'Something is here,' I whisper. The corridor stretches away to our left, and on our right, two steps lead up to the doorway of Lord Rory's rooms. I move towards the door, and the feeling grows.

'You can feel the iron,' she says. 'That's all. It's unpleasant. Although, if you're not a ghost, it shouldn't hurt you.'

'It's more than iron. And don't *say* that!'

'Yes to saying it!' she says, gripping my shoulders. 'If you're not a ghost, Valerie, then we will celebrate what you *are*!'

Her voice is bright and determined, but there are shadows in her eyes, and it won't be nearly as simple as she says. If I am not a Hallowed Ghost, if there's no such *thing* as a Hallowed Ghost, then I am not who I thought I was – who Meg thought I was. Every moment of my life here will have been built on a lie.

Meg leans in, brushing my forehead with a cold, whispery kiss.

'Stop worrying,' she says, drawing back, her voice low and fierce. 'Nothing will change you and me. Nothing in all the worlds there might be out there.'

I nod and reach for the door. The iron rings through the air, but it doesn't hurt. It's not the door making me feel strange, I don't think. Maybe it's whatever Lord Rory is hiding behind it. My skin is clammy, my heart pounding like rain on rooftops.

'Can you open it?' Meg says. 'Do you have your pin?'

I take out the old, twisted hairgrip that we've used over the years to get into rooms, when we don't want to filter through the doors. It's weird, going through walls and doors. Bearable, but too warm and too close, like an itchy jumper that's a size too small.

We've never tried to break into Lord Rory's rooms before. The thought of being discovered is uncomfortable. He's never been unkind to me, but I've heard how he talks to Mrs Peters – I know there's a temper behind those rose-tinted glasses, and I don't really fancy being on the receiving end. I grit my teeth and keep on poking, even as the strange feeling gets more intense. It's like the pull of the river, I think, as my pendant vibrates against my skin. Meg hisses at me to hurry, and the hairpin twists and flicks, and the barrel of the lock spins. It takes about five attempts, but eventually there's the click of a lock opening.

Slowly, my hands trembling, I push the door open into Lord Rory's sitting room. There's a heavy gold velvet settee set before a flickering fireplace, and a vast gilt mirror on the wall shows a whisper of me – dark hair a little wild, my pendant gleaming.

I look back at Meg and take her hand. 'OK?'

She nods, looking a bit pale herself, and I pull her through the doorway. She winces and stumbles, but when she rights herself she looks as excited as ever.

'It's been a long time since I've been in here,' she says. 'I did love our little tea parties, Valerie.'

There were little cakes, I remember, on a stand. And egg sandwiches with the crusts cut off. Lord Rory would ask how my letters were going with Mrs Peters, and he'd listen while I told him, watching seriously. He'd ask Meg how business was going in the Ghost House, which she loved. She'd give him a long, very precise rundown of every guest, and all of their annoying habits. Sometimes he'd bring me a present – a colouring book, or new paints – and Mrs Peters would pop in and out with napkins and fresh candles.

'Let's see what we can find,' I say.

Joe said that I would feel the magic in the Anchors, and now that we're in the room I can definitely sense something, growing stronger by the moment. Meg sticks close beside me, and we tread over the thick carpet to the door that leads to Rory's private dining room. Thick damask wallpaper, and shining trinkets on the mantelpiece; golden candlesticks, glass elephants and ornate little silver boxes. There are glass cases on the walls with rows of little china cups and porcelain figures, all winking in the light. They're beautiful – but they're not pulling at me like the river does.

'There,' I whisper, pointing as the strange vibration explodes into a fire inside me.

It's just a plain wooden door, set into one corner.

'There's something in there.' I rush forward and reach for the handle, and it snaps with static, sending a wire of shock through me.

'Valerie – step back!' Meg twists around me and tries to pass through the door, but it doesn't work.

I brace myself this time and put my hand out slowly. Cold metal, but no static.

I push the handle down, and the door opens silently into a small room, all lined in dark, shining wood panels. There are two workbenches, lit by ornate reading lamps, and on one is a row of tools that look like tiny silver picks and hammers. An old work apron has been flung over one end of it, and there's a small gas canister next to it. Nuts and bolts have been arranged in glinting piles.

On the other bench is a single sturdy wooden box, partially open, and it's casting rainbows over the whole room.

'What is all that?' Meg asks, approaching the table. 'Is it *sparking*?'

'I think it is . . .' I whisper. Keeping one eye on the connecting door, I go over to the shelves and pull the box towards me.

Inside is a thundering, sparkling mass of things that sing of magic and possibility. Old brass bangles, pocket watches, silk scarves threaded with real-looking gold, pens of jade and emerald, and a wristwatch, all heavy with power. The vibration in my chest soars.

I gaze at the objects in the box. A silver pocket watch with ornate loops and whorls engraved on its case; a tiny golden shell on a leather lace; a ring inlaid with pearls.

'It's everything Joe said would be here,' I say, raising my eyes to meet Meg's.

Meg and I stare at each other in silence for a long moment. Joe was right – about this, at least. The wooden floor seems to buckle beneath my feet, and it's only Meg's cool, calm grey eyes that keep me standing.

A door bangs in the distance, and I can hear Lord Rory's voice.

'He's coming!' whispers Meg, hustling up to the door to listen.

I push the box to where it was before, looking desperately around for a hiding place. I have never been able to count on my invisibility the way Meg can. Sometimes a mirror reflects me, pale and gauzy; sometimes a guest just catches a glimpse.

'I think he's got someone with him!' she whispers. 'Come on.'

We edge out of the little workshop back into the dining room, just as Lord Rory comes through from the sitting room. Meg's right; there's someone else with him. She grabs my hand and we sink down by the dresser. I take deep, slow breaths, concentrating on the darkness in the little corner, hoping it will hide me.

Rory is wearing a dark suit under a heavy maroon cardigan. There's a woman with him, her golden hair wound around chopsticks in a high bun. She has freckles over her nose, and her step is light, almost dancing.

'. . . tricked me. I thought the way would always be open between our worlds,' she says. 'I trusted you!'

'You have no business being here,' Lord Rory says. 'How did you even cross over? I blocked the bridge!'

'That block is wearing thin,' the woman says coldly. 'It just took one boy with more power than sense. He's been worrying at it for years. There was a piece of his Anchor in our initial transaction, so I kept an eye on him, and when he finally managed to break through I followed him. You should never have done what you did that day.'

'A boy? What boy?'

'Don't worry about him,' the woman says. 'He won't get far – his magic will have been drained by the journey over.'

'I can't have strange boys from Orbis over here!' Lord Rory says. 'What were you thinking? You should have stopped him, not followed! Any business we had is long past – I need nothing from you now.'

'You need to give the Anchors back to me. You were never meant to hold on to them. You took advantage that day, and took far too much. You must have taken what you need from them by now.'

'As it happens, I haven't,' Lord Rory says. 'I'm still using them. Was there anything else, my dear?'

'What happened to the girl?' she hisses. 'She was not part of the deal!'

'The girl is not up for discussion,' Lord Rory says, his voice becoming low, melodic. 'She belongs here now.'

The woman winces, and turns her eyes from him. 'Are you *fond* of her?'

My ears prick, heart quickening.

'She has power,' he says. 'I've nurtured it all these years, watched it build in that pendant of hers, and now it's nearly time – she's going nowhere.'

There is a silence. I don't dare look at Meg.

'You worked it out then,' the woman says, her voice barely more than a whisper.

'Thirteen, isn't it? A special number, and a special age in the magical community. I have heard it over and over in many of the parts of the world I've travelled.'

'You found other magical places?'

'No,' Rory says shortly. 'In all of my adventures, it turns out there is only one Orbis – and only in Orbis can one find Anchors.'

'What . . . do you plan to do with her?'

'She has so much magic,' Rory says softly. 'Most of the magic in the other Anchors is gone now – I suppose they lose power after a while, without their owners. But hers has been building all these years – that pendant is *full* of magic. I will just siphon it off, every once in a while, and she need never know anything about it. So long as she is here, she will give me all I need.'

'What *is* your need?' the woman asks, her eyes still averted. 'I cannot see that you have used this magic for good, or for much at all!'

'It is magic that kept the bridge closed to you for all those years,' he says. 'And it is magic that stops me from becoming just another ghost in a cursed house of ghosts. It used to bring me other things too – I could travel with it, adventure around the world, bring back riches to shore up this old house – but now it is grown thin. I am trapped here until I have her magic. And that will be any day now!'

'You cannot know her birthday,' the woman says. 'Even *I* don't know that. Even—'

'It is engraved on her pendant, stupid woman,' Lord Rory snaps.

She looks at him, and her eyes widen as he stares at her. The pull in my chest tightens; he's using magic on her, I'm sure of it.

'Come,' he says eventually with a smile, once she is still and quiet. 'Let me show you the way out.'

She follows meekly, all argument forgotten, and I feel like I'm going to be sick. He's a monster! My breath comes fast and everything feels blurred around the edges. Meg is pulling at me, wincing as she does so, but I am dimly aware of us moving through the sitting room and the still-open door and out of his nightmare quarters.

'Quick,' she whispers. 'To our room. Don't even think about it right now, Valerie.'

She swirls about me, hustling us both away from the west wing. I cannot float with her now – every footstep of mine thunders, and the carpets whirl beneath me. Staircases I've rushed up all my life suddenly swoop and bow, and the guttering candles make lakes of darkness that I might fall into.

Meg stays at my elbow, pushing me onward, and finally we ascend the narrow steps to our attic bedroom. The window is open, and the waterfall roars, crashing at the lower levels of the viaduct. I cannot see rainbows or magic, there is no slender arching bridge. Just loops of darkness beneath a slender crescent moon.

'Read to me,' Meg says, pushing the sheets back on the bed with a grunt of effort. She curls up by me on the bed and I tuck my hand under the pillow. I mean to pull out our current mystery book, but Ada's diary comes instead, its soft leather cover falling open.

My eyes sting, but I read to Meg until I can't read any more, and it isn't comforting, but at least it isn't lies.

This whole house is built on lies.

Ada

Today I have had an adventure! I shall have to hide my book even more carefully after I write this. I thought that perhaps I had better not write it at all, only it is a story too magical, too exciting, not to be told.

I walked over the bridge.

I put on my sturdy boots and waited until little Flo was busy making scones with Cook, and I stepped on to the viaduct. The spray drenched me immediately, but I kept going, and halfway along, I saw something out of the corner of my eye: the golden gleam of the magical arch that I had spotted from the riverbank that Monday, but had secretly feared I may have imagined. It was real! I saw that it stretched the length of the viaduct, so I followed it, and when it rose to meet the viaduct itself, I stepped across to it – and continued along it to a dreamland of golden spires and sparkling skies of rainbow stars!

I have not 'lost my wits'. This is exactly what Papa would say, of course, or any reasonable person. But I have not. It was real.

I ventured down towards this magical city,

and into the bustle of people all glitter-skinned and dressed like shimmering rainbow mackerel.

A single small girl saw me. She made me think of Flo. She led me to sit in a park where silver doves murmured, and I told her I had crossed the bridge.

She was very proud; she had just had her 'Anchor dedicated', she told me. Of course I had no notion what she was talking about, and so she explained.

All of the people in this golden, magical city are magicians! Their magic is tied to the Anchors they have about their person. She showed me hers: a little pearl comb that rested against her left ear. She took it out of her hair and let me hold it, and it fizzed in my hand with her power!

I almost wish I had never gone, for then I had to leave. The girl told me that I must never return; that already by visiting, I had changed the course of my legacy. The bridge, she said, was strictly out of bounds. It had been created generations ago by someone like me, who sought adventure – and it had never led to anything but trouble. The magic that existed in her land was a danger to ours.

Her final words filled me with such sadness, and such fear. She saw it all on my face and said if I would wait, she would go and fetch her parents and they could explain it to me better. She ran off, and I saw that in all her panic and excitement, she had left me still holding her comb.

She had skipped off without it, this most precious vessel of her magic, because she was a child, barely older than our Flo, and she had not learned that people cannot be trusted.

I *cannot be trusted.*

I never should have done it, but I couldn't resist it – I wanted its magic. I took the comb with me, and now I shall have to keep it, for I dare not travel back there.

Chapter 10

I wake from familiar dreams of golden streets and bright, winking stars with my heart racing. It's still dark, and rain spatters against the window. Meg isn't here, and sleep won't come any more; my mind is fully awake with everything that happened in Lord Rory's rooms.

I grab my jumper, pull it on over my nightie, and rush down the stairs and out of the front door into the bleak cold of pre-dawn, taking a deep, full breath as soon as I'm clear of the Ghost House. The wind is blowing a gale, and my hair is tossed around my face as I head down, further than usual, to the very edge of the tumbling water. I shiver, looking into its iron depths. No gold, no rainbows. No answers. I turn to the waterfall and start walking, blinking away images of Lord Rory and the mystery woman. I don't want to think about it.

My skin is all goosebumps, and every step is a new decision – part of me knows I should just turn back and incur the wrath of Ted by making toast in his kitchen – but I keep going, and the water changes as I walk. It's faster here, fed by the waterfall, a tumble of white foam against the dark undercurrent. Every now and then there's a glimmer of something like what Ada described; what I have always felt down here. Almost nothing, but not quite. Sparks on the white horses. Violet and indigo against the grey wash of water.

When I reach the waterfall there's a flash deep within the river, not of gold, but a myriad of colours, suddenly revealed and dimming just as quickly, as the sun begins to rise. My skin and clothes are damp; my boots slip against the wet, muddy bank. But there it is: a flash of magic, deep within. Joe was right about everything – and I can't keep ignoring all the things I've learned. Lord Rory was talking about *me* with that woman last night. About my birthday, and my pendant – and all the magic I've got built up in it. She looked so furious with him, before he charmed her. Because he'd taken me.

I ignore the now-familiar thrum of my pendant, and hold one of my hands up in front of my face. It looks just like it did before. Freckled, my skin slightly iridescent in the wan mist of dawn. If I don't belong here, then I might have another family somewhere. A mother and a father; maybe even siblings. And that woman might well know them. I try to picture them in another world, living magical lives together, but that hurts, so I blink the thoughts away and steal between the stones, careful not to stand on any of the ancient burial mounds.

The ground rises to country lanes on one side, and to the viaduct on the other. The tracks are broken and rusted, the bridge itself fissured with deep cracks. I walk along the rails. The metal is rough and cold beneath my boots. I grit my teeth as the bridge leaves the safe ground and looms over the tumbling dark river. It is so quiet up here.

I walk to the centre of the bridge, wondering if I'll catch sight of this magical land. But when I look around all I can see is the Ghost House looming over the river, so close to the waterfall. The light from the windows falls on to the gardens. I imagine my family in there, my *ghost* family playing their games, and I miss them. Why am I doing this when I could be safe and warm at home?

Because of Lord Rory. It's *all* because of him.

I turn, my foot catches on a broken section of rail that twists off to the side, and my ankle turns.

I scream—

Freefall, and a sudden jolt, caught by one hand.

'Hold on!' Joe's face looms over me. 'What were you thinking? Give me your other hand!'

I'm dangling over the abyss. My arm feels like it's being pulled out of its socket, my body hanging precariously. The waterfall thunders and white horses spray up around me. Joe is overhead, on his belly, his face strained.

He tightens his grip on my wrist and thrusts his free hand towards me. I grab at it with my other hand as he pulls, screaming between my teeth as he hoists me over the edge and on to the safe path of the tracks.

'You're OK,' he says, breathing hard, hands on his knees. I roll on to my back and stare up at the sky, my mind a blank hum of everything and nothing. 'You're alive.'

Pulled back from the brink by a boy who I'd thought was as much of a ghost as I am.

Alive.

'You're bleeding,' he says.

'It does happen,' I say, checking the scrape on my arm.

'But you're supposed to be a ghost. Why would you even worry about falling off this bridge? Ghosts would survive that, wouldn't they?'

'Water,' I say, still focusing my eyes on shuffling clouds, my breath tearing through my chest. I feel like I lost something, while I hung there looking up at him; like part of me did fall, and the rest of me isn't ever going to be the same. 'Ghosts can't cross running water.'

'You are not a ghost,' Joe says. He straightens, and the clouds shift and he's outlined in the glowing clouds of sunrise. 'Not even a Hallowed Ghost. You're from Orbis.'

'I know,' I say, pulling myself up after him and following him back over the bridge.

'So you believe me?' he says at last.

I nod. 'Lord Rory . . . I was in his rooms, and a woman came in. They were talking about the stolen Anchors, and she was angry, but he did something to her, tricked her, until she went away.' I blink back sudden, furious tears. 'He took me. And now I don't know what to do.'

'You come back with me,' Joe says. 'But not without those Anchors.'

We enter the cemetery and head towards the crypt, the Ghost House a constant blot on the landscape.

'If you're right,' I say, 'then they all lied to me.'

'Maybe they didn't all know.'

'Maybe,' I sigh. 'But some of them did, I think. They told me stories that they thought I needed to hear, and now it's all falling apart and I don't know who to trust.'

We enter the crypt and sit down on the floor, side by side.

'You can trust me,' he says. 'Tell me what you heard. Who was this woman? What did she look like?'

'I only caught a glimpse. Blonde hair and freckles.' I swallow hard. 'I thought Lord Rory was a kind old man . . . I thought he'd *rescued* me!' There's a long silence. It's so cold in here. In the place where they found me. Where *he* found me. 'He's a liar and a thief,' I say, glaring back at the Ghost House.

'And very nearly a murderer,' says Joe.

The air pops as he talks, and the silver sparks spread over the floor towards me. His words have a strange, rumbling power that sends a storm through the crypt. There's a deep shuddering yawn, and then a crack that splinters into my ears and sends dust showering down over our heads. The stone tombs tremble, and a lichen-covered plaque falls from the wall of the crypt, smashing to pieces as it hits the floor.

'Joe! What's happening?' I press my back against the wall. 'What do you mean, *murderer*?'

'Sorry,' he says. 'I didn't mean to scare you.' His eyes lick with blue flame, behind his glasses, and he takes a shuddering breath, winding his power back in. 'The people whose Anchors are missing suffer terribly. Without their Anchors, they can't control their magic. You see how I am, after I've over-exerted myself. For them it's a thousand times worse. I told you, they're locked in the tower just to keep them from hurting themselves or anyone else.'

'I know. I'm so sorry, Joe. Your pa is in there—'

'And many more!'

'It doesn't seem like it's a good thing, all this magic,' I say, looking from him to my pendant. 'What does it do, apart from make blue sparks and trouble?'

'You're seeing it out of context,' he says. 'It can do anything – when it's properly used and controlled. Back on Orbis, it powers everything. It's in the air, and the water. We learn from a young age to control it, and only to do good with it. How to heal, to hide, to make light. How to grow things and enchant things.'

He cups his hands under his chin and closes his eyes in concentration. After a moment, there's a glow within his palms. He opens them, and a small pale light floats up to the crypt ceiling. It bobs against the stone, revealing the pale green lichen, and slowly fades.

'Not my best work,' he says.

'But magic,' I whisper. A little wiggle of excitement goes through me.

'Magic – and you have it too. You just never learned to use it. When you come back with me, you'll see.'

When I go back with him.

'Do you – do you know my parents?' I say, holding my breath.

'I think so,' Joe says. 'I think their names are Willa and Fed . . .'

Willa and Fed . . .

It starts as a whisper in my mind and turns to a storm.

Willa and Fed . . .

Fed and Willa . . .

'There's something I should tell you,' Joe says. 'They—'

'Stop!' I say. My voice cracks like thunder. The whole

crypt seems to shudder, and tiny flakes of masonry scatter from the ceiling.

'But . . .'

'I'll be back,' I say, and I run.

I run from the crypt, and Joe, and the names of people I don't remember, and the magic that swelled and cracked the ceiling.

It was easier to be a Hallowed Ghost.

Why did I ever want anything more?

Chapter 11

Valerie!

The house is alive with noise when I walk back in, but through all the mayhem one single small voice rings like a bell, cutting through Cecil's storytelling, and Iris's shrieking up and down the landing.

I know whose voice it is.

And I need to find her, now.

Mrs Peters tries to intercept me as I cross the lobby; daylight spills in behind me, and she wants to know where I've been. But I don't feel like talking to her, so I just keep walking. Great-Aunt Flo flutters about me for a while, but I ignore her too, following the voice that feels so familiar, down past the kitchen to the cellar door. The stairs creak, and the fire has long gone out – nobody comes down here at this time of day.

'Ada?' I whisper.

You're here!

The voice that whispers is a boom in the cellar. The candles in the wall sconces flare to life and the fire rekindles, sending a ruddy light through everything.

'I need your help,' I whisper, backing into the wall.

You have magic. I could feel it, more and more – I tried to warn you! I told you to be careful.

'I know you did. I just didn't understand.' I sit on the chaise longue and poke at the fire – though it's roaring now, I still feel cold. 'I know why you've been hiding now. I know what you did.'

There's so much noise, comes the voice. The surface of the chaise longue dips down next to me, though I can't see anybody. *All the time, you are all so loud. I wanted quiet, and so I made it quiet down here. I hid. I thought I could be forgotten. Left alone. And then after all this time, that boy came down with all his sparks and reminded me, and I did not want to be reminded. I wanted to forget!*

'But you can't forget, can you?' I ask, poking at the ash. There's a desperation in her voice that scares me. 'You made a mistake . . .'

In one instant it was done! And it changed everything – there's nothing I can do about it now. It's too late, too late.

The air gets colder, and mist starts to curl over the floor. The fire dwindles as fast as it was lit, and all the hairs on my arms stand up. *What do you want from me?*

'Tell me about Orbis.'

You have read my diary! Ada's voice becomes a whisper. *You already know! You're wasting time. The stolen things, you must return them. Take back the comb, I never could . . .*

The fog drains away, and she's gone, leaving a clinging sense of sadness. Those whispers, that thundering sense of *something* down here – it was always Ada. She's been here for so long, hiding in the dark, ashamed.

'We can fix it, Ada,' I say, but there's no reply. The fire dwindles, and I shiver, before turning and heading back up to the main house – running straight into Meg, who's waiting at the top of the stairs.

'What were you doing down there?' she demands. 'I've been looking for you!'

'I was searching for answers.' My teeth hurt. The room sways for a moment and the mirror on the wall is a flash of light that stings my eyes, showing me nothing of myself at all. 'I found Ada.'

'What?! You *saw* her?'

'Well, no,' I say. 'I heard her voice. She's been hiding,

Meg. All this time, since she stole that comb from the little girl! We need to find it, and all the things that woman brought over for Lord Rory. We need to get it all out of his rooms, and back to Orbis. That's why the star storms are happening – I'm sure of it. There's too much magic here that doesn't belong, and now we *know* Lord Rory is behind it all.' I sway, and everything goes dark for a minute.

Meg stares at me, a look of concern on her face. 'Low blood sugar,' she says. 'Come on, let's have an egg before we save the world.' She ignores my protests, and barrels into me, driving us both down the corridor. 'Nobody can adventure on an empty stomach – it's rule number one – and nothing's going to change in the next ten minutes. If I could eat anything in the world, it would be an egg. Poached, on toast, with lots of butter and salt.'

'Ted says poaching eggs is a pain,' I say, giving in as my stomach rumbles.

She laughs. 'All the better!'

'I love you, Meg,' I say.

She goggles at me. 'What's got *into* you today?'

'I don't know! I just felt like saying it.'

'Softie,' she says.

But she's a little bit more vivid as we head into

the kitchen, a little bit brighter, a little bit happier. It counts, I realize. Whatever else is going on, whatever might change in the future, right now my love for her counts. Saying it out loud counts.

'An egg!' I sing, clattering into one of the old wooden stools by the kitchen counter. Ted looks up from the hob, his face rosy from the steam.

'Oh is it, missus!' he grumbles.

'Poached, please, on hot buttered toast.'

A little wire of static spreads across the counter from my fingers. Fortunately Ted has his head in the fridge, and Meg is watching him hungrily. I frown and clench my hands together in my lap. It didn't hurt, exactly. I felt that tug, though, like I feel at the river.

'Got Meg with you?' he asks.

'We do love a good egg,' I say weakly.

'Everybody loves a good egg,' he says, cracking one into a pot of boiling water. 'About a million of you, all wanting a good egg. And if Ted doesn't get them just right, then there'll be trouble . . .'

'He's talking about himself in the third person.' Meg sighs. 'Always knew he had that in him.'

'I heard that, miss,' he says, waving his slotted spoon in the air.

She laughs, as he scowls in her general direction, and then she goes over to 'help' him, passing the salt, and tossing slices of bread at him for toasting. The whole kitchen is a whirl of movement, of clattering pans and flashes of silver, and the smell of bacon.

I sit and try to enjoy it, but I feel peculiar. I hardly taste the egg. I just about choke it down, watched by Meg and Small, who has wandered through the wall. He's old and grizzled, as high as my chest.

'Hey, Small,' I whisper. I put my arms around him, so that his wiry grey hair tickles my nose. Deerhounds are big as ponies, soft as butter.

'Come on then,' Meg says, when I'm done. 'I'm not entirely sure you're fixed, but it's a start. Let's go and hunt for this comb.'

This house has always been my friend. On the bitterest nights it keeps me warm. Its lights flicker like a heartbeat when I go up the stairs, and the drains giggle when I sing to the mirror. There is always somebody up, somewhere. Meg, to listen. Ted, to make hot chocolate. Cecil to talk to. Even Mrs Peters.

But as Meg and I walk down the corridor now, it gets dark, and the walls seem to creep in towards me.

126

Great-Aunt Flo is in the distance, calling me onward, and there's a gleam in her eyes that I don't trust.

For the first time, the house feels against me. It's a ship yawing at port, its timbers creaking and cracking, and only cold ocean beneath me. Little fissures rush out around me across the carpet, and it smells like burning.

'What's happening?' I whisper.

'There it is!' hisses Great-Aunt Flo, looming back towards us, her lace dress all tatters and scraps. 'The evidence! You are unAnchored and so your magic burns. I *knew it*. Look!' She flicks a finger towards me.

I look down at myself.

My pendant is gone.

When did I lose it? Where?

'Where is it?' I wail, and my voice is purple – it bursts out of my throat in bright bubbles that pop in the air between us, making Great-Aunt Flo's pale hair spiral up from her head. I am swimming, I realize. Not floating, but swimming through the air, and little gold veins glow as I push through; the lifeblood of the house, like I never knew it could be.

'Valerie!'

Great-Aunt Flo winks out of sight, and Meg is beside me. 'What's happening to you?' she demands.

'I lost my pendant,' I say, struggling to land on my feet. I push my palm firmly against the patterned damask wallpaper to keep myself down, and the bubbles are old gold now, a thousand little pendants and none of them real.

'How did you lose it? You never take it off!'

I rack my brain for where I could have misplaced it.

'Someone must have taken it,' I manage, through my teeth. 'I lost my footing on the viaduct and fell. Joe caught me – I thought he was helping me . . .' Even as I say it, I can't bring myself to believe he might have taken it.

Meg shivers, and a tiny silver trickle of water slides down her temple. 'Do you think he stole it from you then, so that he could use your magic to get back over the bridge?'

I shake the unwelcome thought away. 'I don't think so, Meg. I'm not sure it works like that – and his magic is getting better, he doesn't need my pendant.'

Or does he? I try to think, but everything's a muddle. *Can* I trust Joe? And if I do, then who else could have taken my pendant?

Lord Rory?

Tiny dark strands straggle across my hands, and

when I flex my fingers darkness pools in my palms. I take a step back from Meg, holding my arms wide.

'Meg,' I whisper. 'You should go.'

'I will not!' She looks outraged.

'But I can't control it,' I say. My words tangle in my throat, and when they come out they dance with sparks. I clamp my mouth shut, but the darkness is still gathering in my hands. 'I need my pendant, Meg.' In this new light she is a golden shape, her form dancing like the flame of a candle. 'You look different.'

'So do you,' she says. She glances around uneasily. The walls are cracking. 'I think we should go outside . . .'

As she says it, the candles in the chandeliers burst into light. The flocked wallpaper begins to move, like a tide across the wall. I follow her quickly to the stairs, and with every footstep the carpet unravels. Tiny sparks trail behind me and crackle up the walls. When I put my hand on the banister a sweep of gold rushes out. Down the stairs all the portraits come to life, old ancestors turning their eyes on me. Narrow, pinched faces open with surprise, and then the walls around them start to splinter, in sweeping cobwebs that stretch to the ceiling and crawl across the entire lobby.

Guests appear in doorways, their faces shocked.

I make it to the black-and-white-tiled floor. It shatters.

Every single tile is fractured with tiny golden fissures. The reception desk where Leon is sitting starts to skid across the floor with a fizzing, popping sound.

'Valerie!' Leon shrieks, jumping back out of his chair before he gets caught in the sweep of magic. 'Stop it!'

'I can't!' I howl. 'I don't know how!'

Chapter 12

'Valerie!' Mrs Peters comes bounding out of her office. 'What's going on? What's all this commotion?'

'Magic,' I whisper.

'It was you?' Mrs Peters blanches. I see Cecil emerge from the kitchen with Ted. 'You're the one causing the star storms?'

'No!' Meg says. 'Of course she's not. We *told* you about the boy. He came to get back all the treasure Lord Rory stole but he couldn't find it and now he's taken Val's pendant!'

They all stare at me.

'S-s-sorry,' I say, and sparks fly out with my words, shooting up to the chandeliers.

'Outside! Now!' roars Mrs Peters. 'Everybody out!'

She rushes towards me, bearing down, looking

terrified as the floor continues to shatter under her feet. I run out of the main doors and down the steps, through the gravel drive and on to the grass. It shivers and transforms into a carpet of stars.

'Oh my,' mutters Meg. She's stayed by me the entire time, my golden sprite sister. 'You are making so much magic!' She turns in the field of stars, her eyes bright. 'It's amazing, Valerie!'

'All the guests are leaving!' cries Mrs Peters. 'Valerie, please!'

I turn back to her. She's at the bottom of the doorsteps, the rest of my ghost family around her, all the guests fleeing past, their suitcases hastily packed, trailing socks, their arms full of books and toiletry bags.

'I'm so sorry,' I call out.

The sky flashes silver. Meg squeals, and spreads her arms wide, and gravel churns as the guests run for their cars.

'I didn't know!' I call out across the drive. 'I didn't know the pendant had magic. I didn't know *I* had magic! You told me I was a ghost. You told me I was a Hallowed Ghost and we were family and this was home and I believed you – and now the pendant is gone and I can't stop it!'

'You are a ghost! Or you *were* – I thought you were!' says Cecil, stepping forward. 'Lord Rory brought you in and told us you were special. He said we must bring you up as one of our own. As a ghost, with a little *extra* . . . and that's what we did! None of us knew about this *magic*!'

'Where is Lord Rory now? He wants my power, Cecil – I heard him say so! It was probably him who took my pendant!'

'No, Valerie.' Cecil looks worried. 'That can't be right – he means you no harm. We welcomed you, we loved you – we still do!'

'Enough of this,' snaps Mrs Peters, folding her hands together. 'Of course this is your home, Valerie. Now tell me what's going on.'

'I told you about Joe,' I say. 'He says he's from another world called Orbis, and things have been taken from there and brought here, magical things that cause the star storms. He says I'm from Orbis – that I'm not a ghost. My pendant is one of the magical things, and it's gone missing, which is why everything is going wrong.'

'This all seems very far-fetched,' she says, even as the stars pop in the air around me. Her voice sharpens as she turns to Cecil. 'Cecil? Did you know anything about this?'

'No. Nothing of magic, or strange worlds,' he mutters, frowning.

'It was a secret. There are always secrets in families,' says Great-Aunt Flo, drifting over and staring into my face. Her large, brown eyes glitter in her washed-out face. 'Little ones, big ones. Little ones that feel big, and big ones that feel little. Always.'

'You *know*,' I say, looking her up and down. 'You know things, don't you?'

'Certainly!' She smiles. 'Hundreds of years of knowing right here.' She taps her head, and then filters off again, becoming almost transparent as she heads back up the steps into Lightning Falls.

I watch her go. That gossamer-thin look she's got is because she's tired.

Tired from causing mischief? From hiding things she shouldn't?

I turn back to Cecil. 'You lied to me. I thought I was a ghost!'

'Nobody could be certain that you weren't,' he says. 'You walk through walls, and people rarely see you, though you're in their faces. So we made up a legend.

A Hallowed Ghost. Everybody likes a legend. *You* liked your legend!'

'It made me feel special!'

'And so you are,' Cecil says. 'So are we all. It turns out that your difference is . . . a different difference to the one we thought. But how could we have known that there was a whole other world that explained it? To me, you were a ghost. Family.'

'But I'm *not* a ghost. And now there's trouble,' I say. 'The magic is making star storms!'

'We must fix it,' says Mrs Peters. 'No guests, no Ghost House. Rory will sell it off to developers.' She looks around at us, her eyes sombre. 'And then where would our strange family live?'

'I'll stop it,' I say. I take a deep breath and hold it for a while, and the sparks begin to fade. When I breathe out, I do it slow and steady, and I walk, slow and steady, towards my family. Towards the Ghost House. 'I need to find Lord Rory. He needs to explain.'

'I'll come with you,' calls a voice behind me. Crossing the field of stars, his hair crackling with blue light. Joe. 'It's time your *Lord Rory* answered a few questions.'

Ada

Oh, this weight, this weight I am carrying! And from such a small thing! A theft: my one and only, and if I had stolen the moon herself, I think I would regret it less.

I have blinded Father and cursed this whole great house – and all who live here. The groomsman, our caretaker Cecil, our lovely maid, and my most beautiful Florence. I have ruined them all, and all for a small pearl comb that I thought I'd wear, just once, to Father's ball.

It was spectacular, just as it was meant to be. Guests had travelled from London and even further to be with us, and for the first time since Mother's death the air filled with laughter. The guests were in their very finest evening wear: full dresses and powdered wigs, and elaborate face masks. Some with horns; some long beaky noses; some sparkling visors of rubies and diamonds; all of them beautiful. Roger was in his element, playing host in a sumptuous navy coat trimmed in gold braid, his mask winking with sapphires.

There was a banquet first, in the dining room.

The housekeeper, Prudence, had got out all the best linen and crystal goblets, and tall black candles were in all nine chandeliers. The vast bronze-framed mirrors reflected the dazzling light so that it bounced off all the silver. The wooden floor was bright and shiny as an ice rink, and there was a musician playing the old piano by the heavily curtained windows. Father had hired dozens from the local village to bear trays that groaned with food, and the chatter was immense.

After dinner, the ball. And Father drew me out for my first dance! I was clumsy, and he was fleet-footed, his eyes still bore traces of sadness.

'My Ada,' he said with a smile. 'You are so like your mother.'

I bent my head, the comb behind my ear sparked, and the evening turned to chaos! I do not have the heart to describe to you all that happened. Guests ran as sparks rushed out across the floor and up the walls. The chandeliers flared, dazzling spots of light filled the air, and Father stood in the middle of it all, with me.

The magic has blinded him, and we are all in darkness now.

There will never be another ball. I will never dance again. I have brought it upon myself, and – worse – I have brought it upon us all. Roger has taken the comb. He has taken it and hidden it, and he forbids me to ever speak of it again. I do not know what he will do with it; I have never known what Roger will do next. He says he has put it somewhere safe, so that it cannot do more harm. I think we should take it back, across the bridge, but he won't allow it, and the shock of it all has weakened me, so that I am feverish and quite unable to fight him.

To whomever finds this diary, I am sorry. If you have found it, then you know our cursed story. It is all because of me.

Chapter 13

I walk up the steps with Joe and Meg beside me, and as I go I notice for the first time the tiny gold stars that glitter in the stone, the threads of silver in the vast front doors.

'I don't know if you should come in,' says Mrs Peters, standing in the doorway, looking between me and Joe. 'There is so much of this so-called magic! You have already shattered the floor, woken the ancestors in all the paintings! I've never seen anything like it! Besides, Lord Rory has gone out, hours ago.'

'I need to look for my pendant! Perhaps it's in his rooms – you know he fortified the door.'

'That man . . .' She shakes her head, shadows flickering in her eyes.

It's about time someone challenged him, says a familiar voice.

Mrs Peters turns. There's someone in the lobby. She's small, and golden-formed, just like Meg. She tucks herself in close to the wall as I head past Mrs Peters, as if she can still hide from us all.

Ada.

I can feel your magic! says Ada. *I knew there was magic in you. I have never been able to resist its pull. It got stronger when that boy appeared. I could not get hold of him to tell my story – he was a slippery fish! But he awoke something in you, didn't he? And now without your pendant, you are bright as new gold!*

'Did you take it?' I ask. 'Like you took the comb?'

Her figure darkens, and she hunches her shoulders. *No. Not I, this time.*

I think for a moment. 'Your brother, Roger – what happened to him after he took the comb from you?'

She looks over her shoulder, her face pinched with fear. *He hid it from me and I tried to get it back – but that was the year of the flu. I never did cross that bridge again. He was always so greedy, he took that little comb and made a monster of himself!*

'What do you mean?' My voice is tight, my mind racing as her eyes widen. 'Where is the comb now, Ada?'

Roger has it! she bursts out. Wind rushes down the corridor and the candles in the wall sconces erupts into flame. *He has it still! And now your pendant too. You won't find it. He has taken it and marooned you here. He means to take your power, Valerie, and hold on to it for good!*

Roger? She must be confused – doesn't she mean Rory? How does any of this make sense? My skin is on fire, my head throbbing from the effort of keeping all the magic under control, and looking at Ada is difficult; she's glitchy and shadowy, far more than any other ghost here.

Great-Aunt Flo rushes out of the shadows. 'You did it, Valerie!' she cries, grinning. 'You brought Ada out of the cellar! I knew you would. She was hiding, all these long years, ashamed. I could never make her come to me. I *knew* your magic would draw her out – and so it has!'

Florence! Ada claps her hands to her mouth. *Did you take Valerie's pendant?*

'Just like you took that old comb,' Great-Aunt Flo says, defensively. 'I read about it, you know, after you died. I found out all your secrets – and I hid them from Roger. I have missed you so much! I knew Val's magic would draw you out. I wouldn't have had to take the pendant if you'd have just come to me.'

I was ashamed.

'What that man has done is his fault, and only his,' says Great-Aunt Flo. 'He took that magic. He still uses it, you know. And he had other things brought to him, over that bridge of yours.' She looks back at me.

'Roger? But he must be long dead,' I say. 'You mean *Rory.*'

The sisters stare at me, Great-Aunt Flo wordless for the first time ever. And I understand, then, in a flash of clarity that makes the ceiling swing.

'Roger Falcon *is* Rory,' I whisper. 'Which makes him . . . nearly three hundred?'

'He only looks about seventy,' Meg says. 'How is that possible?'

Orbis magic! Ada hisses. *He's used it, somehow, to keep himself alive – our brother is a monster, Florence, and it's all my doing!*

'He's used the comb – and all the Anchors that woman brought over – and *me*?' I say, my words cracking into the air. 'Just to keep himself alive all this time? And you knew it all along, Ada – you knew I was from Orbis!'

Meg clutches my wrist, staring back at Cecil. 'If you're the old caretaker from Ada's diary, then you must have known, Cecil!'

'I didn't know about Orbis,' Cecil says. 'I always thought there was something strange about the viaduct, but I thought he really had just found Valerie, abandoned . . .'

'But all this time, and he's still alive, how did you not wonder about that?' she demands.

Cecil spreads his hands, lost for words.

'It's time we put an end to all this,' says Joe. His voice is tired, his face pale. He's probably using all of his energy just to keep from adding to my star storm. 'Where are all the Anchors now?' He glares at Great-Aunt Flo. 'Where's Valerie's pendant?'

'I lost it,' she says with a wince. 'I took it to winkle Ada out of her shadows, and because I thought Rory would take it on her birthday anyway – he was always wild about your birthday, Valerie, and the power of being thirteen. I thought it would keep it safe for a while, until all that was past, but he must have found it. I underestimated him.'

'You'd better hurry and find it then, Valerie,' says Mrs Peters in a crisp voice. 'If all this is true, we must resolve it, and quickly, before he returns. I mean to have it out with that man.' She waves an arm at the shattered floor, the still-chattering portraits, the sparks that linger. 'What was he thinking? The star storms were ruining business!' She turns on Cecil, and I take the opportunity to dash for the stairs, followed by Meg and Joe.

'Even if we find the Anchors, this won't end well,' Meg hisses as we flee up the stairs, taking them two at a time. 'Lord Rory will discover his precious things have gone and he'll sell the place to developers and we'll all be homeless!'

'We won't let that happen!' I say, as we get to the top of the steps. Joe skids around me and starts down the corridor the wrong way.

'Joe, *this* way!' I say, rolling my eyes as I dash on.

'Sorry,' he says, making a U-turn, his voice snapping with static. The air around him fills with tiny gold sparks. 'Impatient.'

'How are we going to stop him?' demands Meg as we charge on down the corridor.

'I don't know,' I say. 'But we will, somehow. All of us together – one man can't ruin everything!'

'One man can always ruin everything,' she mutters darkly.

'Not if everyone else keeps fighting,' I say, taking

another deep breath as the carpet starts to unravel beneath my feet.

'You'll have family over there in Orbis,' she says. She's afraid – I can hear it in her voice – for all that she encouraged me to discover my past. 'On the other side of the bridge. You're *alive*, Valerie. You're going to go with Joe and leave me behind in a crumbling house with a load of old ghosts!'

'You are my family,' I tell her. We've reached the door and I thrust the hairpin into the lock. 'You can come with us. It will be an adventure, just like you wanted.'

'I *did* want adventure,' Meg says. 'I'm just not sure this is the one I'd have chosen.'

My hands are shaking and sweaty, my whole body throbs with my heartbeat, and I wish she wouldn't keep voicing all my own doubts and worries. I turn to her, just as she puts her hand up to mine on the lock.

'Come on then,' she says. 'Stop messing about. You know how to do this – I taught you!'

Her cool fingers slip through mine. We twist, and flick, and the barrel turns. We're in.

*

The room is deathly quiet, the air stretched thin with tension. Joe is silent as he follows us in. His magic winds about him like silver wire; I can see clearly now how tight he has to keep it, just so that he doesn't do the sort of damage I did. Because he's still recovering from crossing the bridge? Or because part of his Anchor was taken and kept here?

'This way,' I say, heading to the side room and letting us in.

The two benches are unchanged from when last we were here, the box of sparkling things on full view. Joe dashes over and delves into the box, gasping as he pulls out a watch,

'This is Pa's!' His eyes gleam, and silver spangles dance in the air as he speaks. He shoves the watch deep into his pocket. 'There's so much in here – we have to take it all.'

He pulls his messenger bag around and starts to dump things inside, wincing as power snaps against his fingers. I can't see a comb, nor any pieces that might fit on to Joe's binoculars.

'Where's the comb?' I ask Meg, as Joe continues to fill his bag. 'There must be another hiding place . . .'

There's a cold, sharp crack through the air, and then

a familiar voice speaks just by my ear, making my hair stand on end.

Here, says Ada. *Follow me, Valerie – it's here!*

I follow her voice to a little cupboard that has been built into the wall beneath the single small window, and Ada hovers there, her form flickering more than ever.

I open the cupboard, and there's a glitter of gold, and one small comb. Nine tiny pearls at the top of long, sharp teeth, and a jagged nick in one corner, sharp when I rub my thumb against it.

Nothing else. No sign of whatever might be missing from Joe's Anchor. The comb sparks against my skin as I pocket it.

Don't dilly-dally! Be sure the comb gets back where it belongs, says Ada. *Do what I couldn't, Valerie!*

Closing the cupboard door, I turn to the others.

'Quick. Let's get out of—'

The door bursts open, and Lord Rory dashes in, his face flushed with shock and rage, making immediately for Joe and the bag of Anchors.

Joe manages to thrust the bag at me as Lord Rory grabs hold of him.

'Valerie!' Lord Rory says, turning on me. 'Meg! Who

is this boy? What on earth are you *doing* in here?' He holds Joe back with one hand, and their magic tangles around them, making the air hum.

'This is Joe,' I manage, tucking the bag behind me. 'He's from Orbis. You know all about Orbis, don't you?'

'You are intruding!' Lord Rory splutters. 'How dare you! These are my private rooms!'

'Full of Orbis magic!' Joe says, tearing himself away. 'You're using our own magic against us!'

'You took the comb from Ada!' I burst out. 'You've been using magic all these years, just to make yourself live longer! Why would you *do* that – *how* would you do that? Don't you know your sister has been here all this time because of that comb? Don't you care?'

'I wasn't the one who took it,' he says angrily, the frames of his glasses catching the light as he flinches away from me. He doesn't seem to have spotted Ada, who is watching from the corner, and I wonder if he's just spent years pretending she isn't here. '*She* was the one who cursed this place. Ever since she came back with it, ghosts and more ghosts! Father was lucky – all those who died and never came back were lucky. But Ada, and then others, all lingering long after they should – I knew I'd be stuck here as a ghost when I died.'

'What's so wrong with that?' hisses Meg.

'It's unnatural.' Lord Rory shudders as he stares at Meg, and through her to the fireplace.

'That's not true,' I say. 'There have always been ghosts – there always have been. It's not up to you to decide what's right or wrong about that, *Roger*.'

He pales, as if momentarily thrown back to that boy who lived here with his two sisters, and then his mouth curls. 'Taking that comb was the best thing I ever did. As soon as I had it in my hands I knew there was something special in it. And when I managed to prise a piece of it off, I could feel the magic course through me. Not enough to keep me young, perhaps, but enough to keep me young *enough* – to keep me alive. This house always had magic of its own, it comes from the connection to the river, but it's nothing compared to the real thing.'

He looks at Joe, studying the sheen of his dark clothes, the magic that gathers around him. 'I didn't know about Orbis for a long time. I spent many years adventuring, travelling the world, trying to find more objects like the comb. I never did – but then that woman crossed the bridge, and I realized all the magic comes from over the river. She told me Orbis was full of it, that she would bring more to me if I would help her extract magic from the Anchors to add to her own. I was very happy to help, for a price. You were betrayed by your own, boy – your anger has no truck with me.'

'I need my pendant,' I say, drawing his attention from Joe. 'You took it to get power out of it – and I thought you *cared* about me! All the birthday stuff, I thought it was real! You were my family!' My eyes sting as I look him up and down: the tall figure, immaculately dressed, and so familiar. I adored him, but he wasn't who I thought he was at all.

His eyes narrow with rage, his face flushed with it. 'Family! This cluttered, dusty old house with all its clanks and whispers – *my house*, taken over – it is not family. Nevertheless, I took you in. Fed you, clothed you, told you stories – didn't you have everything you needed? Didn't I provide for you? And now you take against me? You stand here with this boy and challenge me? For the sake of *this*?'

He takes a glittering object out of his pocket and holds it up high, out of reach. My pendant. 'I found it, tucked into the stones. Were you hiding it from me? Tricksy girl. I planned on giving you a new pendant for your birthday – you'd have hardly missed this old thing.'

'Of course I'd have missed it!' I shout. 'You're horrible. Why are you *doing* all this?'

'Without the power from these magical things, this Ghost House will fail,' he says. 'What do you think keeps the ghosts here? What do you think keeps this whole pile from collapsing around our ankles?'

'It's not true,' Joe says, staring up at Lord Rory with a frown. He seems weaker, as though his magic is unravelling. 'Your ghosts are here because they belong here. There is magic here, but it's not because of *you* – it's because it was built right next to the river and Orbis. The ghosts aren't going anywhere, and nor is this house.' He takes a step closer. 'You have a piece of my Anchor – it drew me over the bridge, to this house. Where is it?'

'You should give it back,' I say, stepping up to Lord Rory, Meg beside me, bristling with rage. 'It doesn't belong to you. None of it belongs to you!'

'What does it matter?' Lord Rory howls. 'What does this *boy* matter? All these years I've cared for you, and now you'd betray me – this house – for him?'

The words take my breath away, even as I tell myself they're not true. I'm not betraying him, or Lightning Falls. I'm just trying to put things right.

'You *took* me,' I say. 'Why did you do it?'

He snorts, twisting my pendant through his fingers. It takes a huge effort not to launch myself at him and fight him for it, but if I do that he might grab me, we might lose it all.

'Your parents were stupid,' he says. 'They followed that woman and saw what she was doing, and even with all their magic, they had no idea how to fight. It was as though they'd never realized the true power of what they had. They handed over their treasures – their *child* – in exchange for their freedom, and they never once looked back.'

My heart hurts. I back away from him – and my pendant – but his eyes stay on me, and the bag behind my back gets heavy. Any minute he's going to see we have it all.

Don't listen to him, hisses Ada, coming out of the shadows. *It's all lies, Valerie.*

'They'll put you in the tower, I hear,' says Lord Rory, stepping closer to me.

His glasses gleam, and his voice becomes smooth, melodic. His gaze flicks past Ada to his bedroom; he doesn't know I already have the comb. I see Meg edging past him, making for the door.

'With your magic out of control, and your Anchor gone . . .' Lord Rory smiles nastily. 'None of Ted's cooking in there, Valerie. None of the home comforts you've been so used to.'

'This is more important,' I say, though his words have struck hard. It's difficult to look away from him, hard to keep the sense of what we're doing here. Joe steps up close to me, but Lord Rory is taking all of my attention; I can't look away.

'You mustn't go,' Lord Rory says, looking genuinely concerned now, his eyes shining. 'There is danger there, Valerie. That world is full of power. I've been protecting you!'

A little shiver runs through me – my life here *is* safe and it's all I know. I love my home; all that Lord Rory has ever given me.

Walk away, Valerie, says Ada. She walks right up to her brother and lingers next to him, until a shiver runs through him. He may not see her – or want to see her – but he can sure feel her. She looks up at him. *He's using stolen magic to manipulate you!*

'She's right, Val – that's probably what he did to your parents!' Meg says.

I stare from Lord Rory to the pair of them, my mind

fizzing with uncertainty, as Joe takes the bag from me and slips it over his shoulder. The door opens behind Lord Rory, and Mrs Peters strides in, Great-Aunt Flo and Cecil behind her, Iris bringing up the rear. Lord Rory turns with a start, and my head clears as they all squeeze through the door, worry lining their faces.

My family.

With or without Lord Rory, I tell myself. With or without magic. And they need the star storms to end. They need all of this mess that *he* made to end.

'What's going on here?' Mrs Peters demands.

'Now!' shouts Meg, grabbing the pendant from Lord Rory's hand. She rushes past me, heading deeper into Lord Rory's rooms, and Joe grabs my hand and runs after her, leaving Mrs Peters to deal with Lord Rory. With a quick glance back, I can see that my family has lined up around him to help us get away.

'Meg, where are we going?' I ask, as we charge through a tiny kitchen. 'I need a moment . . .' My skin hurts, my insides are full of glass. I thought I was special to him, and until that moment I still held out hope, somehow, that this would all turn out to be a misunderstanding – that he was a hero, and not a villain.

'Out the back way!' Meg calls, as Joe hauls at me. 'Come on, Val – keep moving!'

I take a deep, shuddering breath and charge with Joe through the kitchen, pelting through a door and down a narrow, darkened flight of stairs. I've never been this way – it's completely unfamiliar – but Meg charges ahead, and Joe and I follow, until the rumble of the waterfall pounds all around us and I realize we're in the tunnels beneath the old house.

A memory stirs. Meg and I did come down here once, but Mrs Peters found us and there was a lot of trouble, so we didn't come again. The river cuts through the tunnels and we follow it out of the shadows and into a pelt of rain.

Footsteps ring out behind us, and Meg flounders as the roar of water booms. 'You'll have to go on without me,' she says, hovering, worried-looking and pale. 'I can't go in that river.'

My heart clenches for her. 'You don't have to,' I say. 'You got us out of there, you got me moving when I was stuck. We'll be OK – you don't have to come.'

There's a bellow from the house. Lord Rory. He will have discovered the Anchors are gone – perhaps even the comb. A sliver of fear rushes through my spine, and my stomach rolls at the thought of having to face him again.

'You go.' Meg pushes my pendant into my hand. She's held on to it all the way, even though it's always been so hard for her to hold on to anything for that long. 'Go, Val. I'll keep Lord Rory distracted.'

I stare at her. Our adventure is falling apart – I never wanted to do this without her. But Joe pulls me away through the rain, and we run to the viaduct, where he stops and unfolds my hand.

'Come on,' he says, taking my pendant and looping it over my head.

A sheen of silver-bright washes through me. I breathe easy for the first time in what feels like hours as the snap of magic calms.

'Let's do this. You can see Orbis. Then you can come back, if that's what you want. Meg will be here when you return.'

'Your Anchor – the missing bit.' I stare back at the house. 'We didn't get it, Joe!'

'So maybe I'll come back too,' he says with a crooked smile. 'But we need to get going now, Val. Come with me. See your other home.'

The grass shivers beneath my feet; the whole hill feels like it's quaking.

'My parents did abandon me,' I whisper. 'They just handed me over and ran away. That's what you wanted to tell me that night, isn't it?'

Joe holds out his hand. 'You don't know the truth. And you won't, unless you come with me.'

I reach out and take his hand, and my vision blurs with horrible panicky tears at the thought of all I'm leaving behind, but I don't look back this time.

I stare into the rain, and brace myself for Orbis.

Chapter 14

The viaduct looms over us, mountain-high, snapped rail tracks slippery with rain. Joe is soaked through, and so am I. Massive cracks run down the loops of stone, and I can't see anything magical on the other side.

It can't be safe.

Nevertheless, Joe ploughs on to it, the bag of Anchors swinging against his back. I follow him to the very centre, and then I make the mistake of looking back at my life, all small on the other side. The house, all lit up; the cemetery in darkness behind it. Am I really going to step on to a golden bridge – just like Ada did, all that time ago? She was so brave, to do it alone, no matter what came afterwards. Can I really follow in her footsteps?

Yes, I can. To break the curse of the Ghost House,

and this pearl comb that glows warm in my pocket.

I hear faint shouts and cries as Lord Rory dashes out around the side of the house, Mrs Peters following behind. Rory looks up to the viaduct, and for a split second his eye catches mine. The look on his face is pure venom. Mrs Peters is shouting something, and the air blurs around her; perhaps it's Ada, or Great-Aunt Flo, but Rory ignores them all, and runs across the gardens towards us.

And, suddenly, Meg is beside me, barely visible in the fog. 'We need to go!' she shouts. 'Quick, not a moment to lose!'

'Meg!' My heart thrills at the sight of her.

'There's the bridge,' Joe says. 'Look down . . .'

Tatters of a rainbow stretch across the darkness; tiny sparks glint through the rain.

'It doesn't look very reliable,' I say, wincing.

'It isn't!' says Joe.

He reaches for my hand, and I take it, pulling Meg in close to me, and we hurl ourselves off the viaduct.

The rainbow rings like glass when we land on it, quivering beneath our feet. It's wide over the river, but it has no railings, and for a moment I daren't move; it's tricky enough just to breathe, standing on a barely there strand over the fiercest part of the water. Meg squeals, closing her eyes and clinging on to me.

I frown at her. 'Meg!'

'Whatisit?' she breathes, eyes still closed, feet pressed together.

'You're warm! I can feel your fingers!'

'Come on,' says Joe. His white hair is plastered to his skull. 'We need to keep moving – it's not safe . . .'

Meg blinks at me, and I grab her hand and haul her after Joe along the bridge. Every step is another ring of glass in a different note, a pale warp of colours that wraps around our feet.

'What's it made of?' I whisper, keeping close to Joe.

'Mostly luck, these days,' he says. 'Hurry up – he's still behind us!' We run a little further, and then Joe adds, 'It's a shame that we couldn't find the comb.'

'I have the comb!' I tell him.

Joe comes to a stop and wobbles, and the bridge wobbles with him. 'You found it! You have *Ursula's comb* in your pocket?' His hair stands up on end with static, and the bridge vibrates beneath our feet. 'That's amazing!'

'We're going to fall off if you keep doing that!' I

160

shout, my stomach rolling as I try to keep my balance. The river rushes below us, but he's clearly not thinking about that. He's flickering all over with magic.

'You've got the single most important piece of Orbis magic in your skirt pocket!' he howls. 'That comb is *legendary*, Valerie. It belonged to Ursula – she was the daughter of one of our most powerful families. Without it, *all* the magic of Orbis began to dwindle. That's why your Ghost House is so crazed! The more magic on your side of the bridge, the less in Orbis. The more unstable the bridge, and the house too . . .'

'But it was taken three hundred years ago!' Meg says. 'How will it make a difference now?'

'Ursula is still alive!' shouts Joe over his shoulder, turning to run again. 'Well, we think she is. In the tower.'

'All this time later?' I ask, following apace. 'Do people in Orbis normally live that long?'

'No,' he says. 'And I'm not sure whether she's really living, not after all this time. But *something* is up there. Nobody can get to the highest levels of the tower to find out what – the tower is unstable there. That comb could change everything!'

Meg clutches my hand harder as we pick up our pace,

slipping as we run helter-skelter over a rainbow mist of nothing, and the air gets warmer as we follow the curve of the bridge. It veers to the left, and when I look up I can't see the viaduct overhead any more. Below us now is sparkling white sand, and over our heads are stars in a bright, daylit sky that glows with the pink of sunrise. The bridge dips down before us into golden hills over a broad city, sand-pale buildings arranged around a river, which reflects all the light of the sky. There are white marble bridges, and others that spindle over the river in threads of shining silver. Tall, slender towers rise up at intervals throughout the city – between them more bridges interconnect, making a skywalk.

'Wait,' I whisper.

Joe turns to me. 'What's wrong?'

The sky lurches overhead, and my legs tremble. I'm miles up in the air on a thin gold strand, heading into a whole new world where everything will change.

Beneath us, the river has changed. No longer a grey heaving mass, now it's a bright mirror of light.

'Valerie,' Meg whispers.

She is as terrified as I am – I can hear it in her voice, though I can't turn to look. She's only here because she loves me.

'I don't know if we should come with you, Joe,' I say. 'You have all the Anchors. You can take the comb – you don't need us.'

'Yes I do,' Joe says. 'You can't turn around now. I promise, it's going to be OK.'

'We have to keep going,' says Meg. 'We can't stay here, and we can't go back – Lord Rory was just behind us.'

As she says it, the bridge begins to veer dangerously from side to side. Someone else is using it. Lord Rory.

'Come on!' says Joe. 'We can't let him catch us on here . . .'

We hurry on, light and quick. My heart is still thundering, but the air is warm, and I glance over my shoulder to see Meg, bright behind me, as we make for the steps that lead down to the green hills. As we fly down them, they ring out in a descending scale that rings through the valley and echoes through the towers that reach for the sky. Six golden, rainbow-flickering towers – and one that funnels like a strobe of darkness to a moody, swirling, thunderous sky.

Orbis.

Chapter 15

'Welcome to Orbis,' says Joe.

Magic swells all around us, and every breath is a million particles of the strange star dust that filters down over everything. Joe's hand is firm as he pulls me away from the bridge and on to a wide, golden pavement, by the side of a smooth-running river.

Brightly dressed people throng the riverside, and there are stands selling little round sugar cakes and replica towers made of pale wood. In the distance, someone is singing. A dozen small children are gathered around an old woman who is making miniature pink clouds with a long, slim wand of willow.

My blood is racing. The pendant vibrates at the end of its gold chain as I take in all the wonder of this world that could have been my home, and suddenly all the tiny flecks burst into light. My hair blows back, and the pavement bows beneath my feet.

'Valerie!' Joe takes a step back. 'What are you doing?'

'I don't know!' I say, and my voice hums with a thousand strands of power. It feels a bit like my whole body is singing, and the world has got a whole new set of colours.

'It's a lot of magic, is what it is!' He frowns, stepping closer. 'It's your coming of age! You must have already turned thirteen.'

'No – my birthday is next week . . .'

'But it isn't, is it? How would Lord Rory know your birthday?'

'There's a date, on my pendant.' I hold it up, and it flashes in the sun, making sparks run down my arm.

'That's the date you were given your Anchor – four weeks *after* you were born! He got it wrong, Valerie!' He glances back towards the bridge. 'All the magic that's been building in you – it could never fully come out while you were over there, where magic doesn't belong. You turned thirteen, but it didn't mean anything until you were here! We need to get away from all these people. And you need to stop all *that*!'

There are tiny rainbow shards in the air between us,

and every time I breathe out, there are even more. I giggle, and a swoop of them rise up and land in his hair. It doesn't feel scary, like it did when I lost my pendant at the house – it feels alive, and exciting.

'Valerie!'

'He didn't know when my birthday is!' I can't stop laughing, though it's not really funny. 'He waited all this time, and he got it wrong!'

'Calm down,' Joe says, brushing sparks away. 'We're going to attract attention!'

'Joe?' says a voice behind us.

'Now look what you've done,' Joe whispers, looking over my shoulder.

I turn to see a woman with fiery red hair, dressed in a silvery cloak that catches all the falling starlight. She's like a beacon; it's dazzling to look at her.

Joe smiles. 'Hatch!'

'Did you try to get over the bridge again?' She looks from him to me. 'You shouldn't get caught up with him, you know. Trouble, he is. Keeps all of my guards busy.'

'I'm glad we found you,' says Joe. 'I thought I saw somebody crossing from the other side . . .'

The woman shifts, putting her hand on to the hilt of

a sword that's tucked into her belt and glancing up at the hillside. 'Really? That seems unlikely, Joe – I could do without wasting time.'

'There *was* someone,' I say. 'A man – he was tall . . .'

'A tall man,' says Hatch drily, looking me up and down with grey eyes. 'How helpful. Who are you? You look familiar.'

'She's my cousin, from out of town,' says Joe, whisking me away. 'Hope you find that man, Hatch!'

She stares after us, then shakes her head and starts up the hill towards the bridge, calling out to a pair of guards, similarly dressed, who were stationed by the river's edge.

'That'll keep them all busy – and Lord Rory too, hopefully,' says Joe, dragging me through the crowds. 'Hatch is the Chief Guard – she'll stop him, if anyone can. We need to get to the tower—'

'Wait!' I tug him to a standstill. 'Where's Meg? Did she make it off the bridge?'

'I don't know,' Joe says.

I realize with a panic that I haven't seen her since our encounter with Hatch. 'Meg!' I shout, making more rainbow sparks.

Several people turn, and Joe grabs my arm.

'We can't stop here,' he hisses. 'Come on.'

Joe pulls me onward, over warm copper pavements, past houses that dazzle in every colour, and bridges that twist high over our heads. The towers are slender, pale marble structures that reflect the golden sky and the myriad rainbow sparks that fall from the stars.

I blink, because it's bright, and because there are hot tears in my eyes. And then the stars swish down from the skies towards me and pull me away from Joe and hold me tight.

'Meg,' I breathe into her. 'Oh, *Meg*.'

She pulls away from me and lifts my chin with one sparking finger. 'You're all right,' she says, her voice a curl of golden ribbon. 'We knew it wouldn't be easy, kid.'

'Don't call me kid,' I protest, with a wobbly smile. 'I'm so glad you're here.'

'I'm glad I'm here too,' she says. 'You'd be in a complete mess without me. This is some adventure you've got us into. This place is like a dream, Valerie!'

'You've been exploring without me? I was worried – what did you find?' I ask.

'I got excited! There are towers in the sky, Valerie – they taste like hope and wishes!'

I stare at her. Or try to – it's quite difficult in her current form. She's a smatter of gold stars in the air over the shallow stone steps that lead down to the river.

'It's made you a poet?'

'So much magic, Valerie,' she continues, ignoring me. 'I think that Joe was right – every one of these people has magic. It funnels down from the sky and covers the whole world! Except one of the towers is all in darkness. I couldn't get close. It's like a little island of gloom, right in the centre of the river, at its widest part, and no bridges. Even the sky is like a hole of darkness.'

I nod. 'I could see it from the bridge . . .'

'That's where we're heading – it's Ursula's tower,' says Joe. He hefts the bag on his back. 'My father's there, and so is . . . so are your parents. It was charmed so that no magic could escape it, only it's become unstable over the years. It was never made to hold so many.'

'That's why it's so dark?' I ask.

'The charm acts like a dampener, to keep all their unAnchored magic in. It's horrible,' he says.

'And . . . they've been in there all this time.' My mouth is dry. 'They just handed me over, and came back to *that*?' I gaze at the ominous tower.

'My ma never thought they were guilty of stealing

the Anchors, and she said they never would have abandoned you,' Joe says. 'But the thefts stopped after they were arrested. Nobody ever knew what had happened to you. Fed and Willa had lost their own Anchors – they couldn't explain what had happened. Over the years the guards tried to get back over there, to look for the stolen things and the "lost girl", but the bridge was warped – Rory's doing, I'm guessing – and it got impossible for them to cross.'

'*You* could.'

He shrugs. 'I was one small person, pretty determined – *and* there's a bit of my Anchor over there. A bit of my magic.' He tucks his binoculars under his shirt with a huff. 'The main thing for now is to return all these others –' he pats the bag – 'and once your parents have theirs back, they'll remember—'

'That they had a daughter,' I say, and it feels bitter in my mouth. 'And now she's all grown up.'

Meg is lingering close to me. 'It was all because of that woman,' she says. 'The one we saw with Lord Rory. *She* is the thief. Who was she?'

'We'll find out,' Joe says. 'Come on.'

Fear winds up my spine, but something has changed since I stood trembling on the bridge. Magic is everywhere here, and it's in me, and for the first time I feel like I know exactly who I am. Not a Hallowed Ghost, but a girl from Orbis, with magic all of my own – and it all might still be complicated, but I won't miss this. My parents are in the tower. Ursula is in the tower, and she's been waiting for hundreds of years to be reunited with her comb.

I start to follow after Joe, but there's a commotion as a woman rushes over the nearest bridge towards us.

'Joe!' she shouts.

Joe blanches and takes a step back. 'Oh, no,' he whispers.

The woman gets closer. She's dazzling, dark hair snapping with magic, red cloak flying out all around her as she runs.

'Who is that?' I ask.

Joe is looking at the ground as if he'd quite like it to swallow him up.

'That,' he says, 'is my ma.'

Chapter 16

Joe's ma doesn't say another word, just looks me up and down, eyes widening, and then takes each of us by the arm and marches us back towards the bridge. Meg spirals up into the sky with a giggle and a promise she'll find us later – and I just have to watch her go, pulled along by this steam train of a woman.

'Excuse me,' I say, wriggling to get away.

'No, thank you,' she says, loosening her grip only to tuck her arm through mine. 'You're coming with us.'

'Just let it happen.' Joe sighs. 'She'll only be cross for a minute, then she'll be feeding us cake.'

'That's what you think,' Joe's ma snaps. 'You have really done it this time.'

She drags us through glimmering streets that get narrower and narrower, until we round a corner into a little residential courtyard, the ground tiled in intricate patterns. Balconies line the upper windows, striped awnings sheltering them from the sun.

A shout breaks out on one of those balconies, echoed by a dozen voices, young and old. I hear the pounding of feet on stone steps. People burst on to their balconies, and all around us is a chattering call:

'Joe! It's Joe!'

'Where've you been, Joe?'

'She's going to *kill* you, Joe!'

This last is howled by a little girl of about nine in a spotted dress, hanging on to the railings, leaning forward on her belly, her whole face lit up with delight. An older woman pulls her back, tutting, and tucks her arms around the girl, both of them lingering to watch the drama unfold.

Joe's mother rounds on us, finally breaking her silence.

'Where *were* you, Joe?' she demands. 'No. Forget I asked you. You'll probably lie, and we all know where you've been anyway – you tried to cross the bridge again!' She takes his face between her hands and looks at him, turning him this way and that. 'You're all thin! And you've been gone so long. What happened?'

'I made it over. And I got lost on the other side, for a bit,' he manages, his voice muffled as she throws her arms around his neck.

I watch as he lowers his head to her shoulder for just an instant, before she moves away, and relief turns once again to anger.

'What were you thinking?' she demands. 'Of course you got lost! Hatch has warned you off trying a million times! You'll end up in the tower yourself!'

'I don't care! I was *never* going to stop trying. I made it over – and I found the Anchors!' he says. 'Dad's watch, and so many others, all hoarded in one place. And Valerie, Ma.' He sweeps his arm out to point at me. 'I found *Valerie*.'

She turns and stares at me, and there's a long, awkward silence. My feet remain stuck to the little mosaic tiles. She's so loud and vivid. My heart is beating too fast, my eyes prickling. I've never had a rush hug like that in my life. Never had a mother haul on to me, hug me, tell me off. I had Meg, and Mrs Peters, and they are all I ever needed, but *this* – what Joe has – is something different – something that I didn't even know existed until right now. What must it be like to have a mother like *that*?

'Valerie,' she breathes eventually. 'It really is?' She looks to Joe, who nods like his head's not attached properly. I glare at him, as his ma takes my hand and leads me towards one of the buildings. She pauses outside its red door. 'I *knew* there was something, from the moment I saw you. Come on, both of you. Explaining to do, immediately.'

We enter the cool shadows of the house. The entrance is a small, dark space with a stone tiled floor. We head up two flights of narrow stairs that cling to a whitewashed wall, and finally pass through a heavy wooden door into a small apartment. The windows are mostly shuttered, but the doors to the balcony are wide open, and the little girl who shouted down comes rushing at us now.

'JOE!' She barrels into him.

'El.' He grins, wrapping his arms around her. 'Little sis. You're still speaking to me?'

She pulls herself away and shakes her head, then looks from him to me, frowning. Their ma heads towards the back of the apartment, calling for us to follow her into what turns out to be a wide, sunny kitchen, where she's joined by the woman who was out on the balcony. Her dark hair is caught with silver at her temples.

'Aunt Frida,' Joe says.

'Joe. We've been worried.' Her gaze lands on me. 'Who is this?'

'I'm Valerie,' I say.

'Valerie,' she says, her eyes lingering on me just a second too long. 'Well, well. I'm sure Callie has a lot to say to you, Joe.'

'I'm sure she does too,' he mutters, giving his mother a wary glance.

'You really found the watch?' Callie asks, as soon as we're all settled at the kitchen table. Light pours in from the balcony at the front, the shadows of the wrought-iron bars cutting the room into sections. It's warm, and the air is full of tiny darts of light. 'Show me, son?'

'Here,' he says, pulling it out of the bag.

It gleams as he sets it on the table. El reaches out to touch it, but Callie stops her. The watch has a white face with three gold hands: two to tell the time, and another that turns in a tight, glitching motion.

'You got it back!' Callie whispers. She stares at him. 'You mustn't ever run off like that again, Joe – after an argument. You must never let things fester.'

'I didn't fester – I went to fix everything.'

'But your father wouldn't have wanted that! You risked so much – you're far too young to get involved in all of this.' She looks from him to me. 'And what you've found, Joe . . . after all this time. I can't quite believe it.' She shakes her head. 'Can it really be baby Valerie?'

Frida snorts. 'Of course it's Valerie. It's clear as day, she looks just like Willa.'

She's so certain, so bold with it. My heart clenches, and I have to look away from her.

'I knew she was from Orbis, as soon as I saw her,' Joe says. 'Though she took some convincing.' He smiles, as I keep my eyes fixed on the table and all the gleaming Anchors. 'We found everything over there – even *Ursula's comb*.'

There's a stunned silence. I shrink back into my chair; it turns out it's pretty excruciating sitting through someone else's family drama, even if you've got a starring role.

'El, go to your room,' Frida says eventually.

'Aah, Auntie Frida!'

'Go on, love,' says Callie. 'It'll not be for long. We need to talk to Joe and, ah, Valerie. You can take a biscuit with you . . .'

El rummages for what seems like forever in a tin on

the side, before taking three iced biscuits and sloping slowly off to her room.

There's a long, strung-out silence, as Joe lowers the bag carefully to the floor.

'You found the comb?' Frida asks in a hushed voice. 'Are you sure, Joe?'

He nods. 'Val has it.'

I reach for my pocket, but then Frida waves a hand. 'No. Wait. Don't get it out now. Who knows what will happen?' She looks between Joe and me, and then to Callie. 'What are we going to do?'

'We're going to return it all!' Joe says. 'Why are we wasting time?'

'Wait,' says Frida, holding up one hand. 'There's no rush. We can't just charge into Ursula's tower with all of these stolen things and expect the guards to take care of everything. We have to think for a minute. You're back, and you have returned that which was lost, but there will be questions, Joe. You did something illegal, however well intentioned.'

'Illegal?' I ask. 'What was illegal?'

'Crossing the bridge is forbidden,' says Frida. 'It was known that it was a weakness for Orbis, and that the world on the other side was dangerous. After Willa and Fed were discovered and arrested, the guards made an attempt to cross and recover the stolen Anchors, but the bridge began to glitch. It was never meant for regular travel, and something had broken the power of it – even Hatch couldn't fix it.'

'So everybody stopped trying,' mutters Joe.

'We couldn't risk more lives trying to get them back,' Frida says. 'There is a malevolence on the other side of the bridge. It thwarted all efforts, and we nearly lost good guards in the river over there.'

'It was Lord Rory,' I say. 'He broke your bridge, to keep you all away. And now he's followed us, so actually there is a rush!'

'Who is Lord Rory?' Callie demands.

'He's the one who had the Anchors,' Joe says. 'He's been taking power from them. We got Hatch watching at the bridge for him, though. He'll have to get past her if he wants to find us.'

'That's no easy feat,' says Frida. 'But who is this man? How did he manage to take power from our Anchors – to use it against us?'

'We think he had someone from Orbis helping him,' Joe explains. 'A woman. Valerie overheard them talking.'

Callie pushes her chair back from the table, grabbing a glass jug and filling it from the tap. She goes to the shelves over the sink and takes down four cups, putting them all on to a tray, and bringing it over to the table. The jug glows like a lamp as it's set down, and when Callie pours from it into the little cups I realize it's the water. It looks like it's full of stars, and I can't help but hesitate when everyone else drinks.

'It's OK,' says Joe. 'Just water. It's different here.'

'Everything's different here,' I manage.

'Valerie. It must be strange, after all this time – in that other world,' Callie says in a careful voice.

I nod.

'Has Joe told you what happened?'

I shake my head. 'I just know I was . . . taken.'

Frida nods, with a smile that doesn't quite reach her eyes, staring at me. 'The very image of Willa, you are. It's a terrible thing, that you were lost for so long.'

The storm that's been building in my chest cracks with thunder. I put my hand to my locket and breathe through it, trying to act like this is all just your normal sort of conversation, in your normal sort of day.

Only the whole world is changed. And so am I.

'What happened?' I ask. 'How did I get caught up in

180

it all? Why would anyone take a small child over that bridge?'

'They took you everywhere,' says Callie slowly. 'They were quite the adventurers . . .' She smiles, shaking her head. 'When they came back over the bridge without you their magic was all in disarray. There was nobody else with them. They still had some of the Anchors on them. After they were arrested, the thefts stopped, so everyone thought it *must* have been them – and that they had sold you too.'

'*Sold* me?'

'But you didn't believe that, did you, Ma?' Joe says.

Callie shakes her head. 'I knew your parents. They loved you so much,' she says. 'They were tricked, somehow. Overpowered. What can you tell me about this woman you overheard?'

I try to remember. 'She said she'd followed Joe over the bridge and went to see Lord Rory. She asked about the Anchors and me, but he turned her away. He manipulated her somehow, she stopped arguing with him . . .'

'He got rid of her, because he didn't need her any more,' Joe says. 'He had all these Anchors – and he had you.'

x

181

I have so many questions. My parents names clamour in my mind, *Willa and Fed*, *Willa and Fed*, and there's so much I want to know about them. I take a breath to ask, but then there's a hammering at the door, hard and insistent.

'Calliope! Frida! Are you there?'

I freeze. That voice is familiar. El pops her head in.

'It's Auntie Miriam! Shall I let her in?'

'No!' I whisper.

Everyone stares at me.

'That's *her*!' I look at Joe. 'That's her voice – it's the woman who was with Lord Rory!'

'Miriam?' Callie turns pale with shock. 'Miriam wouldn't have done all this. She was distraught when Fed and Willa were arrested.'

'But she was jealous of them too.' Frida's eyes spark. 'She wanted to travel the world as they did, looking for magic, but her own power wasn't strong enough. If she had found a way to take magic from others' Anchors for herself, she might have done it, Callie – there never *was* enough suspicion of her.' She flinches as the hammering starts up again. 'She handed them over, and presented herself as the heroine! And she got away with it, all this time!'

'Callie!' shouts Miriam. 'I know you're home, what are you up to in there – is Joe back with you?'

'We have to go,' I whisper.

Joe nods and scoops up the bag, putting the watch inside.

'El, back to your room,' says Frida. She turns to the rest of us. 'Callie, you should go with them, I'll let Miriam in, and you can head out through the balcony . . .'

Callie ushers us to the glass doors, treading soft and quiet over the tiled floor, and we listen as Frida marches to the front door.

'Miriam!' she says in a loud voice. 'Sorry to keep you waiting. You look very flustered – come in!'

The door bangs and we tiptoe out on to the balcony, creeping over the metal floor to the steps and rushing out through the courtyard. Callie is fast, and for a few minutes there's no time for thinking – we're just rushing through alleyways, making heads turn, before emerging into the main street that lines the river.

'OK,' breathes Callie, slowing to a casual stroll. 'Well. If you're right about everything, we shall have to sort it out.'

'If we return their Anchors to Willa and Fed, they'll

remember what happened,' Joe says. 'We need to return the comb too . . .'

'What a sight that will be,' says Callie with a smile, looking up at the dark clouds that seem to have gathered permanently over Ursula's tower. 'Ursula's magic returned, at last. It should stabilize all our magic, Joe. And Orbis's skyline will be as it was long ago. Free of that awful dark funnel.'

Chapter 17

We make our way past a small park where violet-collared doves flutter around a marble fountain, and then down another narrow street, this one mostly in the shadows of taller towers. Callie steers us on to the main street and down to the river. It's wide and fast-flowing, narrowboats painted red and pink and green bobbing up and down on golden water. The colours here are far beyond what I could have imagined, and the dying sunlight filters down through myriad sparks that dance in the air. I keep an eye out for Meg as we go, wondering if I'd even see her through all the magic.

'The river is amazing,' I mutter to myself, before tripping on the edge of one of the shining tiles that paves the river walk.

'It's where our magic comes from,' Joe says, his

eyes bright and full. He must have missed it so much. 'Anyway –' he snaps out of his reverie as we head through a tunnel beneath one of the pale stone bridges, away from the river – 'keep your wits about you. Not everything that is magical is good for you.'

'It isn't magical to have to rely so much on one thing,' I say, fingering my pendant.

'No,' Callie says. 'We never used to have to be so tied to our Anchors, but since Ursula lost her comb, the magic here has been unstable. And people's Anchors are pretty much all they worry about, ever since these all went missing years ago.' She looks around, and I follow her gaze to see a couple of guards, strolling behind us. 'Come on!' she whispers.

'There are quite strict rules for using magic,' Joe says, as we pick up our pace while trying not to look suspicious. 'It's like having a weapon. The more powerful you are, the more dangerous it is. You're not really supposed to be going around sparking – it can upset things.'

'I saw that earlier, in Lightning Falls.' I wince.

'That was just mild stuff,' he says. 'That sort of thing happens all the time here, if people aren't careful. Say one of your sparks landed on a lamp post, it might turn it into a frog. Depending on your mood. Might turn it into a crown.'

'Anything's possible?'

'*Anything*,' Joe says. 'You can use it to keep yourself young, though that takes a lot of magic so you basically can't do anything *but* remain young. And you can alter things around you. Someone turned the houses along the promenade into swans once for a dare, but they went swimming off down the river, and the guards had to catch them and herd them back to be returned to their original form. The people who had been inside those houses were never the same again . . .'

'So if you get something wrong, it can be reversed?' I ask.

'Usually. It can leave after-effects. And it has to be reversed by the person who did it in the first place, which is tricky, because some spells take all the magic you have stored up – none is left for turning things back to what they were again, until you've built it back up again.'

'That's what happened to you after you crossed the bridge,' I say to Joe, as we bustle after Callie. 'But it was easier on the way back?'

'It wasn't just my magic we were using.' He smiles.

I tilt my head and stare at him.

'Your magic!' he says. 'It comes easy as breathing, when it's going right. Thank goodness we got your pendant back from Lord Rory.'

'He was waiting for my birthday.' I shiver. 'Or what he thought was my birthday.'

The dark tower is close now, and the thought of Lord Rory sends a dart of dread through me. All those years I thought he loved celebrating my birthday – loved *me* – and he was just waiting for my power to grow.

Callie ushers us forward, down some ornate steps, and we emerge into a narrow street, where laundry hangs from upper windows, and tiny shop doors tinkle as people enter and leave. Children sit on doorsteps, and there are little huddles of people talking. The buildings themselves are narrow, with faded wooden shutters closed to the daylight. Joe is quick as he weaves through the shoppers, keeping his head down low. I follow him, my breath fast.

'Watch out!' cries a familiar voice. A smattering of golden stars, and Meg is here, her still-surprising warmth going through me as she gets close. 'He's coming!'

I look back, and through the crowd I see a familiar

figure. Tall, and slope-shouldered, marching through the crowds, looking hungrily about at the people who dazzle with magic. Lord Rory. A blonde woman walks at his side.

'Quick!' I say. 'He's here!'

'And Miriam's found him,' says Callie, tugging us behind a wall. 'Those two . . . I'll keep them busy. You get that comb to Ursula.'

'I'll help!' Meg says, throwing herself at Lord Rory.

He howls, taking a step back and stumbling into the railings, and Joe and I take advantage of the pandemonium.

The tower is in the very centre of the river, twists of dark metal that stretch needle-sharp to the sky. It's like a little piece of the magic of this world got cut out here. The sky directly above is a grey swirl of clouds, and no light shines on the tower. It digs its roots deep into the river, and the golden water breaks around it, lapping an oily blackness up its walls.

The water rolls over our ankles, biting cold. It sucks at me, tries to draw me down. I hesitate.

'This part of the river is always hungry,' Joe says. 'It's because of the unstable magic that comes from the tower – just keep your focus on your pendant.'

The water sloshes up my legs now. The closer we get to the tower, the colder it is, and the feeling penetrates not just skin and bone but my whole self. Joe is striding ahead, his feet kicking up a demi-tide of black water.

Behind us, a shout goes up. I turn as the guards start to run after us. Callie calls to them, drawing them back just as a great ringing breaks out all around – an alarm, sounding from all the bell towers. Joe doesn't look back, just lurches on faster and I follow. He hauls himself up on to the slick dark stone of the tower steps, reaching behind for me.

The sky cracks over our heads, and lightning forks down to the river. The crowd of people on the promenade draws back as the water begins to seethe, and flickers of light rush up the sides of the tower. Joe hesitates, looking back.

'Ma will be in trouble,' he says.

'What shall we do?' I ask.

'We've come this far,' he breathes. 'She'll be OK. She always is. Nobody's going to hurt her.'

'Let's go then,' I say, scrambling up beside him. 'We can do this.'

And this time it's me, holding out my hand, taking the first steps inside.

The tower is full of darkness – it creaks, and every step lurches beneath our feet. Joe trips on the doorstep, his knees buckling, and I put my arm through his.

'All right?' I say.

'I hate it in this tower,' he says. 'Always did. I can feel the magic draining out of me. And my father is here . . . I don't know what he'll be like. I haven't seen him in so long.'

'But we're going to fix him. You have his watch.'

'Yes,' he says. And he sets his shoulders, and together we march to the vast marble desk that looms up out of the shadows in the far corner.

'I'm here to visit my father,' he says to the guard who steps forward, his voice brusque.

'You made all the alarms go off, young man! Who's this with you?' The man looks up at me with a frown on his face. His beard shimmers with strands of silver, and his amber eyes are keen as he searches us both.

'A cousin. We've already explained it all to Hatch – she said it was fine.'

The man raises his eyebrows. 'Did she now?' He sighs, and turns to a cupboard, hauling out a thick book. 'You'll have to sign in. And if you're lying to me, Joe, it'll be your head on the line.'

Joe turns a little pale, but he manages a smile, and takes the pen from the guard.

Chapter 18

It's dark and cold in the tower. When we first arrived in Orbis I was dazzled by all the light and colour; the absence of it now is a wrench in my chest. There aren't windows in the stairway, only tiny slits too high to see out of.

But I grew up in a Ghost House. It takes a lot to frighten me.

'Where's your dad, Joe?' I ask, as we wind our way up the floors.

'We need to find Ursula first,' he says. The walls around us contract, sending ice whickering up to the very highest peak. 'She's at the heart of the storm. The tower protects the outside from all the unstable magic by cutting it off, but the inside – well, you can see. Once she has her comb, it should get better, then we can go to the others.'

He looks a bit doubtful, and it does feel hard to believe. The comb is so small in my pocket, and this tower is such a vast, creaking thing. We charge on anyway, and I bite back a shriek as the steps rumble beneath our feet, shearing into two with an enormous crack. We press ourselves to the wall, and suddenly Meg is beside me. She doesn't say anything – she just spirals ahead of us, a point of golden light in all the darkness.

'Meg!' I'm so relieved to see her. We follow her up, past floors that echo with the calls of men and women, and the clank of chains.

My parents are here somewhere. Have they spent ten years missing me? I wanted that, I realize, as I clamber up behind Meg, mist now rolling down over our feet. I wanted them to have been wondering about me, as much as I wondered about them. Now I only hope they're still in one piece. That their Anchors are in the bag Joe carries, and we can prove them innocent.

If they're innocent.

'Stop!' comes a roar from immediately behind us. 'Where do you think you're going? Stop, now!'

Joe and I skid to a halt. We're on a landing that

circles around to a single doorway. The guard who let us in scrambles up the steps behind us, out of breath, his eyes snapping.

'What's going on, Joe? You said you were coming to see your pa – you know you shouldn't be up this high.'

'We have the comb,' Joe manages through chattering teeth.

'The comb?' He moves towards us.

'Ursula's comb,' Joe says. 'We found it. We just wanted to get it back to her.'

'Show me!'

I dig the comb out of my pocket with shaking hands and hold it up for him to see. It's tiny. The smallest sparkling thing, ten golden teeth and nine smooth round pearls.

'Stop them!' comes a shout. It's Miriam, with Lord Rory just behind her, his eyes glinting with rage, and Hatch bringing up the rear. 'Thieves! Stop them!'

'What have you done now, Joe?' demands the guard, quailing before Hatch's glare.

'These two have deceived you all,' says Lord Rory in his smooth, melodic voice. 'The girl is my niece. She and your boy here have made off with some very valuable items that are quite unsafe in their hands. We are only here to restore them to their rightful place.'

'How could you do it, Aunt Miriam?' Joe says. 'How could you take all those things? You took *Valerie*!'

'This is Valerie?' Hatch demands in a sharp voice.

'My niece,' says Lord Rory. He steps out and around Hatch, facing her down, a flare of light going through his glasses. 'I cannot thank you enough for your assistance, dear lady. As I explained before, she has had her head turned by this boy and filled with a lot of nonsense. I am here to get her back. Any comb she has is just her own. She's a fantasist – we have never been able to trust a thing she says!'

'Liar!' I shout. 'This comb belongs to Ursula!'

Hatch looks between us, wrapping her fingers around the hilt of the sword in her belt as she drags her eyes away from Lord Rory, who winces as if he's been stung. 'I can't see how she can make things worse,' she says slowly, shaking her head as if to clear it. 'If Valerie would like to use her *fantasist* leanings to reach the top of this tower, she is very welcome to try.'

'It's too dangerous!' says Miriam. 'No one has seen Ursula all this time. Who knows what will happen? The whole tower could come down on us!'

'We should have known,' Joe says coldly. 'When

your hair got brighter, and your house grander. We should have known you'd misused magic. What did he do – siphon some of it off for you? How was it worth all of this?'

'He told me no one would ever know!' shouts Miriam. 'He said he could take magic from them and nobody would ever know! A bit for him and a bit for me, is what he said. I didn't know I'd been followed! Willa and Fed came over the bridge behind me, and they had Valerie with them – and he overwhelmed me. He overwhelmed us all.' She backs away from him, never quite looking him in the eye. 'He already had some magic, perhaps from the comb. He used it – we were all dazzled by him!'

'And yet here you stand beside him,' Hatch says. 'Are you still dazzled?'

'He can do that.' I find my voice. 'I felt it earlier, when we were trying to get away from him. It was hard to look away . . .'

'I don't know what they're talking about,' says Lord Rory, bristling with impatience. 'I *demand* the return of my niece.'

'Oh I think not,' says Hatch, standing between us protectively, carefully avoiding his eye. 'I know the name *Valerie*. The whole of Orbis knows her name – her parents whisper it daily. I think we'll let them try with their little comb.'

'Hatch! We can't let them up there now – it's not some kind of game!' cries Miriam, and she sounds genuinely frightened. 'For goodness sake, that's my nephew! Who knows what kind of monster he'll find up there!'

Hatch doesn't move.

'Come on,' hisses Joe.

We turn our backs on them and run.

The steps are slippery with ice, and black rock is sheer on every side. It's narrow up here, and the banister is a fine thread of silver that looks as though it could break at any second. Meg winks out and it's all darkness, as my feet come to the end of the steps. A single door stands before us on a tiny landing. I take a breath – there's nowhere else to go – and push down on the handle.

A shiver of magic goes through me, and the door opens with a screech. Dark mist pushes back against us. Joe staggers up next to me into a single, spartan room with one window, and dusty floorboards, and a small figure just discernible in the far corner.

'Ursula?' My voice is a whisper that sends sparks of light through the dark tumbling air. The comb is still in my hand; its teeth have pressed into my skin.

'You have it? asks a small, dry voice. The darkness lifts as Ursula comes towards me, a small girl still, as if she's been frozen in time without her comb. 'It's really my comb! It's been such a long time – hasn't it?' She pushes her dark fringe out of her eyes, and my heart pangs at the confusion there.

'Ada is so sorry,' I say, tears rushing to my eyes. 'I know it doesn't change anything . . . It was taken from her before she could return it.'

I hold it out, but there's a sudden shout behind us and footsteps sound on the stairs. Lord Rory clatters up, his skin gleaming. 'Give that back to me!'

He launches himself at me, and I stumble back into the wall, cracking my head, the comb tight in my fist. Joe lunges for him, but Rory lashes out, sending him toppling down the tower steps with a horrible clatter.

'Stop this!' I shout at Rory.

He towers over me, his skin a dazzle of tiny sparks. His sunglasses are like rose-coloured mirrors. He kept himself alive all this time with this magic, and his rage is a physical thing – I can feel the heat of it coming off him as he stands between me and Ursula, acting like she's not even here.

One small girl. Small still, and he doesn't care what this has done to her. What it does to me, or to Joe. To any of the people in this tower.

'Give it to me,' he hisses, grabbing my wrist.

I fling the comb, and it spins over his shoulder, landing on the cold, dark floor.

A small hand reaches out and takes it. A flash of white light bursts out around us, making the room shudder. Lord Rory lets go of me and shouts, and then darkness falls, and silence.

'You returned it, after all this time.' Ursula is the single light in the tower. The comb gleams in her hands, and her smile is the brightest thing I've ever seen, as the light travels through the tower, out of the window.

'Does it help?' I blink back tears; it's a bit like looking at the sun.

'Everything,' she says. 'I wondered what it would feel like, you know. All these years . . . I did try to let go of it. But I could feel it out there. I could feel everything he did with his power. I could feel that he used my magic to bully others, and all I could do was wait, and hope.'

'What will you do now? Will the clouds go? Will it all be better?'

Will my parents be better, when they have their Anchors?

'Oh, yes!' She grins. The stone of the tower brightens around us. 'It will. This was my home, you know. It has always been my home, though it changed over the years, even as I stayed the same. It was the most beautiful tower. There was a garden at the top, and little fountains. Do you suppose it could be like that again?'

'If it's what you want,' I say, watching as she tucks the comb in behind her ear. I turn to Lord Rory. Stunned, or just momentarily blinded by the light, he's sitting slumped under the window. 'What will happen to him?'

'Oh,' Ursula says. 'He has lived his life many times over. I don't suppose he'll manage much longer – especially if we can take his stolen magic from him. We'll put him in the dungeon. Hatch?'

The guard rushes into the room with a clatter of boots and drawn sword, Joe behind her with the bag of Anchors. She rocks on her feet at the scene in front of her.

'Ursula!'

'Look! We have it back!'

'We do?' Hatch's grin is just as wide as the girl's as she takes in the comb, and the brightness that unfurls from it, changing everything. 'Look, Ursula – look out of the window!'

The darkness around the tower is lifting, the sky turning to the same dusky pearl as the rest of the world.

'You stayed all this time,' says Ursula. 'I'm so glad you're still here, Hatch.' She holds out her arms, and Hatch swings her up in another clatter, holding her close.

'It was my job to protect you,' she says in a gruff voice, blinking as she sets her down again. 'You used all your might, and all your magic, to keep you small while you waited – I decided I'd wait with you.' She turns to me and Joe. 'So you brought it back. What an adventure you've had, Joe. Your mother is beside herself. We must find your father immediately.' She turns to me. 'Valerie. Your parents too.'

'Do they know?' I say. 'Where I was – what happened?'

'It will have been a confusion,' Hatch says, raising her glittering sword slightly as she eyes Rory. 'Without their Anchors, much of the last years will have passed in a blur for them. But I can feel their power in this bag of Joe's – we can fix it.'

'Not . . . everything,' I say, stalling. The comb and Ursula were easy; they were for Ada, and for the whole of Orbis. Seeing my parents doesn't feel nearly so simple.

'No magic can change the past,' Hatch says finally. 'But you do have a future, and so do they.'

'Could you take this away?' Ursula asks, indicating Lord Rory.

Joe drops the bag at Hatch's feet. Lord Rory stirs. He looks from the bag to Joe, pulling himself up. Hatch pulls the bag away, and Rory howls in frustration, faced with her sword.

'You,' he says. 'All this time, and one boy to ruin *everything*!' He turns his gaze on me. 'You had it so easy, my dear. I looked after you, made you what you are – and now you think you can stop me?'

With shocking speed, he stretches out one bony hand and tears the binoculars from Joe's neck, then turns and hurls himself out of the window.

'No!' roars Joe, rushing after him and flinging himself out into the sky.

'Joe!' I scramble across the floor. The light over the

river is a strange, flashing green as night falls, and the charm that blocked the magic falls away from the tower. I perch on the edge of the window. Joe is out there, hanging from a Meg-shaped spool of golden stars.

'Meg,' he gasps. 'If he shuts the bridge, I'll never get my Anchor back! Let me go!'

'Into that water? No!' she says. 'Valerie! Jump – I'll catch you!'

I look back. Ursula and Hatch are watching transfixed, the bag between them.

'You'll make sure you get the Anchors back to them?' I ask.

'No, Valerie!' Ursula says, rushing towards me. 'You mustn't leave now – I have heard your parents whispering your name, in the darkest of nights. They've been waiting for you!'

My heart pounds. I have wanted this moment for so long – to know how they look, who they *are* – but I can't leave Joe to face Rory on his own, without his binoculars.

'I'll come back,' I say, dropping off the window ledge, stretching out my hands. Meg catches me, and the three of us dip slightly as we cross the river, but she never lets us touch the water. She drops us all on to the path, just as Lord Rory pelts towards the bridge, heading for home.

We turn our backs on the winking stars of Orbis and charge after him up the steps to the rainbow-glass bridge. A tiny *ping* ricochets across it as we start across. Lord Rory is ahead of us, and he's not being careful. The whole thing could collapse at any moment.

'I'll go ahead,' Meg calls out. 'I can warn the others.'

The bridge sways. Sparks break out around Joe, but he doesn't slow. We slip and slide, as it starts to yaw from side to side. Ahead of us, Lord Rory has reached the shore. A blur of motion is all about him: Meg. I see the porch lights of the Ghost House snap on in the distance.

'Valerie!' Meg's voice is thin and reedy across the roar of the river. 'Hurry! He's doing something to the bridge!'

The bridge begins to sway more violently. I grab Joe's hand, but the motion is too much, and the rainbow cracks beneath my feet. I stumble and Joe smacks into me. There's a tearing sound that fills my head, and then we fall together into the raging water.

There's just time to take in Joe's shocked face as he slams into the bank before I'm torn away from him, driven deep into the dark, the sound of that breaking bridge still ringing in my ears as my chest begins to burn.

Chapter 19

I picture a woman, my mother. She looks like a cross between Meg and Mrs Peters, and she's standing on a dark shore, emerald stars winking above her. My father is next to her, his hair a tangle, his face blurred, the shards of a rainbow in his hands.

It's a dream. A dream of Orbis, of parents lost. I kick hard to get my head above water, but my limbs don't work properly. It's too cold and too fast.

'Joe?' My voice echoes into nothing; all I can hear is the surge of the tide. 'Meg?' The water twists and turns me, pulls me under, and I collide with something. It's Joe, unconscious and sinking, a little spool of silver bubbles coming off him.

I clamp one arm around his chest, kicking furiously, my pendant glowing, until we've surfaced. We are moving backwards through the water now. In the distance I can see the lights of the Ghost House, but the torrent of river is taking us further away.

'Meg!' I scream.

'Don't you dare give up!' comes a great roar, over our heads. 'I've raised the alarm so you had better *fight*, Valerie! I will never forgive you if you let yourself drown after all that we've been through.'

I never saw a ghost cry before. Meg is crying, silver tracks down her cheeks. She looks utterly terrified. 'Find something to hang on to! . . . MRS PETERS! TED!'

The bank is just inches away, but it's rushing past quickly, and Joe is slipping. We head towards a bend in the river and we're dragged down; it's a fight just to get to the surface again. I'm half drowned, my breath is like fire in my chest, and my pendant isn't glowing any more, but I pull on every fibre of my being and force us back up, coughing and spluttering, scanning the undergrowth coming at us for roots, branches, anything. It's treacherously smooth – there's nothing to cling on to. But the river is slower here, and we're not fighting the tide any more. I tip my head back and we float for a while. The stars are smaller here, pinpricks in a shifting sky. Just as beautiful, in their own way.

'*VALERIE!*'

I jerk, suddenly feeling again just how cold and battered I am.

'Valerie!'

Something smacks into the water just ahead: an oar.

I reach for it, catching it as we fly past.

I look up with bleary eyes to see Mrs Peters on the riverbank at the other end of the oar, hauling us inshore, her body braced against the weight, heels digging into the scrubby grass on the bank. Cecil is shouting at her side, trying to help and failing to get a grip on the oar. Her face is set, her breath coming out in a growl as she digs harder, pulls harder, until my shoulder bangs into the riverbank.

Ted appears out of the gloom at a run. He grabs the oar, and Mrs Peters drops to her stomach, reaching forward.

'Valerie, I swear,' she hisses, grabbing my arm and hauling me out, inch by painful inch, as Ted leans over and pulls Joe away from me.

'Let go, Valerie,' Ted manages. 'I've got him . . .'

I let go of Joe's cloak, and Mrs Peters hoists me up out of the river, and then I am on the riverbank in the

silver moonlight, coughing and spluttering, Mrs Peters'
arms tight about me, Cecil beside us. Ted backs up
beside us, dragging Joe by his shoulders. He drops to
his knees beside Joe and checks his pulse.

'He's all right,' he says. 'Got a conk on the back of
the head, looks like – he's lucky you were there to save
him.'

'Where's Lord Rory?' I shiver as Mrs Peters pounds
on my back. I pull away. 'Stop that, I'm fine!'

'You are a wretched worrying child!' she snaps.
And I see it then, in her eyes, that same look that Joe's
mother had.

'I'm sorry,' I manage, staring at her. She hauls me up,
with a deep huff that might be frustration – or relief. 'I
didn't mean to worry you.'

'Don't go falling off bridges then!' she says. 'Really.
As if I'm not old and worn enough with looking after
you all . . .' She stoops to Joe, and I crouch beside him.

'Wake up,' I say. 'We made it.'

'The bridge,' Joe whispers. He opens his eyes. They
are huge, his skin a sheen of silver, just like mine. 'He
broke the bridge. We won't be able to get home . . .'

'It's still there, maybe we can fix it,' I say, as Mrs
Peters and I help him up. She marches over to Ted,

muttering something about hot chocolate. 'Are you OK?'

'I think so.' He winces, putting his hand to the back of his head. 'I can't believe we're back here. I never even got to see Dad . . .'

'We will,' I say, rather uncertainly as the bridge makes another *ping*ing breaking sound. 'At least we're still alive – I thought we were both going to drown!'

'You used your magic,' Joe says, with a faint smile. 'I felt it.'

'I didn't realize it was magic.' I frown. 'I was just trying to get us out of there.'

'That's how magic works,' he says. 'When you need it most, it just sort of happens. But where's Lord Rory?'

'We locked him out of the house!' says Ted. 'Leon and Great-Aunt Flo and that other one, Ada, are holding him off . . .'

'He's got Joe's Anchor!' I say.

'His Anchor?' asks Cecil.

'Magic,' I manage. 'He's got Joe's magic. He'll use it . . .'

Ted curses and sets off for the house at a run, Mrs Peters and Cecil beside him.

'Come on you two! Joe, I found your glasses!' She

thrusts them at him. 'We need your help!'

She is still Orbis-golden bright. She flits up into the sky as she heads back to the Ghost House. It looms up ahead of us, lights blazing, chimneys belching great towers of smoke. Someone's lit every fire, and every candle, and I can see the figures of my family out on the steps. Ada, Great-Aunt Flo and Iris are standing firm against the closed door, while Leon, Cecil and Ted restrain Lord Rory, who flings himself at them, lashing out. He's smaller, somehow, and paler, as if he's worn thin. But there's a shine of something in his hand, and it's strengthening him slowly and surely, sending copper lines of power through his arm.

Joe's power – from the binoculars he stole!

'Come on.' I put my arm through Joe's. 'We can do this.'

'Yes,' he says.

He's ashen, stumbling into me, and as we reach the gravel drive he loses his footing entirely. I strain to keep him from falling as his knees buckle. It's too much, I realize. All the bridge-crossing, and now without his Anchor – he needs it back, and that missing piece too.

'You wait here,' I say, easing him on to the edge of the drive. 'I'll deal with him.'

Joe smiles at me. 'To the rescue once more,' he says. He shudders as bright static rushes out over the ground around him, and I turn to Lord Rory, still wielding stolen power nearly three hundred years after he first took Ursula's comb from Ada.

'Enough!' I shout. I don't put my fingers to my pendant; I just keep it centred in my mind as I flex my fingers. Everyone stops to stare, but I keep my eyes on Rory. 'You can't win,' I say. 'Not even with Joe's Anchor.'

'No?' snarls Rory. 'You think I need this trinket to fight you?' He crushes the binoculars in one hand, and tiny shards of wood and copper fall to the floor. He flings the remains out to the hedges that divide the cemetery from the gardens, and they spark as they fly through the air, before landing in darkness.

'Why steal the Anchors if you didn't need them?'

'Oh, I needed them,' he says. 'But a little goes a long way. And I've had a long time to gather power.'

'Ursula said you won't last long without her comb.'

'She doesn't know I still have a part of it.' He taps the metal frame of his glasses, where a tiny pearl winks.

'You took them apart!' says Joe in a harsh whisper. 'Our Anchors are made in the old forges, and that's

213

where they go back to after people die. Nobody ever exchanges parts!'

'Well I did,' says Rory. 'There is no sense in you having power – no reason I shouldn't. The whole world of magic is base and unfair, and your traditions have no place here. This is my home.'

'Not only yours,' comes a voice behind him. Ada, standing on the threshold with Great-Aunt Flo. She doesn't glitch, or turn to shadows. She doesn't hide in the corner, she stands strong by her sister, and her voice is firm. 'It never should have been yours for this long. We're not supposed to live forever, to wield our power forever, Rory. What are you frightened of, that you build your defences so high, with stolen magic? What life is this, lived at odds with everything around you? You have forged yourself out of iron – for what? There is no joy in you – there is no hope. You are just . . . existing, long after you should have left.'

'Like you ghosts?' he sneers. 'Lingering on, mostly invisible, unable to eat or drink or ever leave this house? I saw it all, once I had the comb. I saw you never left. I saw Florence too, in time. A ridiculous half-life! I never wanted that! I travel! I am free to go wherever I want. I can mix in the finest circles. I wanted Lightning Falls to be a grand old house again, a renowned estate, not a ridiculous tourist attraction.' He looks at me, and his eyes sparkle. 'With a little help from Valerie here, it is all possible.'

I feel the pull of that gaze, the reach of it down into my stomach, and it's all I can do not to go towards him.

'I think you've done enough, seen enough, brother dear,' says Great-Aunt Flo softly. 'Your time is up.'

'Let's see then,' Lord Rory says, his influence on me faltering as he faces his sister. 'Let's test my power against hers, shall we? The power of dozens against that of one small girl.'

'Two small girls,' says Meg, joining me.

'Four,' says Great-Aunt Flo, standing at her side with Ada.

'And one boy,' Joe says.

'You are just ghosts!' Lord Rory snarls. 'Just the shadows of people who used to live here, a long time ago. And one small girl, and a boy who has been without a part of his Anchor for so long, he doesn't even know what it was like to have real power!'

Iris comes to join us. Cecil and Ted are still barring the main door, and Mrs Peters is in the bushes, still searching in the darkness for whatever remains of Joe's binoculars.

'I think you'll find there's power in all of us,' I say. 'But we're not going to use it to fight you.'

'No?' Rory laughs. 'What will you use it for then?'

'I'll just take back what you stole,' I say. 'Bit by bit.'

I put my fingers to my pendant, and I think of all the birthday parties he held for me. All the years I sat across from him while he asked how I was were years stolen from my parents, and the attention he gave me was only ever about the power I had inside. He watched me grow, from behind his rose-tinted glasses – but he wasn't the only one watching. I've *never* seen him without those infernal sunglasses, casting a rose tint on everything.

It all clicks into place.

I know exactly where to strike.

Chapter 20

Pink glass shatters as I draw on bright new magic to end his hold on us all.

'No!' Lord Rory screams, grabbing for the fragments, his form instantly shrivelled, lips curling to reveal blackened stumps for teeth. I keep my eyes on him, my fingers tight around my pendant, and, piece by piece, I pull the sparking magic off the frames of his glasses. He backs into the door, but there's nowhere to go, and he has no power of his own; everything he stole is coming unravelled.

Tiny particles zip through the air, landing in my palm. A screw; a shard of glass; a sparking chip of jade. He yells, and clutches the frames to his face, but I keep going. A miniature golden cog, a diamond, a spool of copper wire – and there's nothing he can do to stop it. They collect in my hand, sparking and fizzing, and lighting the air between us.

It's Ada who reaches out and takes the frames in the end. He doesn't even try to stop her, just staggers on the top step, his face thin, hair turned to wisps. As she throws them to the ground, the storm breaks. A massive, sparking storm – golden chaos, stars and great zipping whorls of light that bounce up to the sky, in pink and green and yellow.

The house shudders, and its facade splinters as magic spills out in every direction. Ted, Leon and Mrs Peters hide their heads in their hands, turning away, but the ghosts and I can see everything. Every crack of lightning, every beam of light. The bare frames of the glasses bounce the rest of the way down the steps, and when I pick them up the final pieces crumble into my hand.

'The house!' Meg says in a hushed voice, staring up at the shattered stone. 'What have we done, Valerie?'

Leon and Ted rush down the stairs, a dazed and crumpled Rory between them, as the porch begins to tremble. We stand way back, watching as bright light breaks out between the bricks, spreading over the whole house and up the chimneys until the whole Ghost

House is alight. For a dizzying moment it feels like it might untether and float up into the sky; like the whole thing was only ever built on magic. The chimneys belch purple smoke that fizzes in the air.

And then, as we watch, a shower of small things starts to tinkle to the ground. Tiny hammers and chisels. Pieces of wood that maybe used to be parts of a workbench. A small gas canister explodes out of one of the chimneys, and an old work apron slowly drifts to land on the bushes at the edge of the gardens.

'My workshop!' Lord Rory gasps, wringing his bony hands.

'You've been evicted,' says Meg, with a look of wonder on her face. 'The house has got rid of all the things you used to do your horrible work!'

Now the house settles, quiet and dark but for the candles in the old chandeliers. It looks just as it always did, except that perhaps the stone is just a little lighter.

'Clever house,' I breathe, as Meg grins beside me.

'Clever old Ghost House.' She gives the nearest wall a little pat, and for one single moment everything is still – but this isn't over yet. There's a new commotion behind us. A singing, ringing sound that takes me right back to Orbis, and all its golden magic.

I turn to see that beneath the viaduct, the rainbow bridge is whole once more, shining beneath the moon, and there are several figures moving slowly across it, their shadows stretching out behind them. Joe takes a step towards it, peering into the gloom to try and see.

'You need your binoculars,' I say.

'Here,' says Mrs Peters, coming over and tipping a handful of fragments into Joe's hand. 'I found most of the pieces . . .'

'And I think this is yours too, Joe,' I say, pulling out a shard of copper that Rory stole, and handing it to him. Joe stares at it. 'Can you put them back together? Will they be OK?'

'Probably,' he says. 'Let's have a go . . .'

He holds up the battered remains of his binoculars with a wince, and his magic starts to build; first of all a stuttering, wiry thing, then full and blooming as all the tiny bits of copper and wood leap together with a clatter and a fizz. For a moment he's lost in a blaze of light. Then the light fades and he turns to me with a grin, holding the binoculars in his hand.

'You did it!' I say. 'How does it feel?'

'I can't describe,' he whispers. He is brighter, fuller somehow, his skin glittering. 'Let's test them out.' He holds the binoculars to his glasses and looks through them at the figures crossing bridge. 'Oh,' he says. 'That looks like trouble.'

I squint, trying to see through all the magic that's still snapping and sparking all around us. One of the figures is much closer. It leaps from the bridge and rushes over the gardens towards us, a slipping, shifting darkness against all the clamour, closer and closer until it staggers to a stop in front of us and I see her clearly.

'Joe!' It's Aunt Miriam, the woman who left me here with Lord Rory, all those years ago. Her hair has unravelled, and her breath comes short and fast. 'You're all right! You have your binoculars – but what has happened here?' she asks, staring up at the house, and then to the pieces of Anchors in my hand.

'You,' Lord Rory snarls. 'You should never have come back here.'

'I should have done it long ago.' She blanches at the sight of him – so gruesomely transformed without his magic – and then turns to me. 'I made a terrible mistake – I'm so very sorry. Your parents followed me, you know. They could tell I was up to something. And they brought you with them. They were always risk takers. Adventurers! Once they were here, there was a massive row between us – they could tell there was Orbis magic in the house, and then they saw the Anchors I'd brought. They would have stopped me – it all would have been over – but *he* came out.' Her eyes glitter as she glances in Lord Rory's direction. 'He was so reassuring. So calm. He manipulated us, charmed us, using that stolen magic. He told us we could return to our lives – we just had to leave the Anchors behind. He dazzled! It was like being spoken to by a god. He let me keep my Anchor as payment, but he took your parents', and he said you'd be better off here – he'd seen the raw power that is in a small child, the bright magic within you. I was barely aware of anything. I didn't know what I'd done until it was too late.'

'You weren't charmed all those years,' snarls Joe. 'You could have returned for her. You could have told the truth when you got back to Orbis!'

'He'd taken their Anchors – they were barely able to walk in a straight line. It made no difference to them, whether or not they'd done it. I vowed to come back for Valerie, but he used his stolen magic to warp the bridge.'

'How could you?' Cecil says to Rory. 'Cutting a child off from her parents.'

'You were easy to fool,' says Rory in a dry whisper. 'You thought she was one of you!'

'She *is* one of us,' says Great-Aunt Flo. 'She is family, more than you ever were.'

'You let her parents take the blame for all the things that had gone missing,' Joe says to Miriam. 'And you left all those Anchors behind . . . You even took a piece of mine!'

'I know,' says Miriam. She looks between us both. 'I don't expect you to forgive me . . .'

Her voice trails away as more people step off the bridge. Coming closer, dark shadows against the bright sky and the river. Hatch and Callie, and Frida, and a man who must be Joe's father – I can see the likeness, even though his face is worn and haggard, his white hair straggling to his waist. His eyes are on Joe, who lets out a little gasp and runs to him. Behind them are a man and a woman, who I don't know. I can't look straight at them, my heart is pounding, my eyes blurred and aching, but they keep coming towards us – they are real, solid people, not wisps of maybe.

My parents.

I blink, and make myself look. I didn't think I remembered anything, but now that they're in front of me, there *are* traces of familiarity, glints of memories. A large nose over a grey-speckled beard, and a thatch of hair that never behaved – my father, who laughed like thunder, and told me stories of strange faraway lands with purple skies. And my mother, her dark eyes shining, her hands clutched tight together at her stomach, as though she's holding herself back with everything she has. They're dressed in the shimmering rainbow-dark clothes of Orbis, and their skin has that same sheen in the moonlight that mine does.

They're staring just as hard as I am, but nobody moves. It's like nobody knows what to do next – except Hatch.

'You –' she charges at Lord Rory and Miriam – 'are both under arrest. You're coming with me.'

'I can't go over there!' Rory splutters, as she hauls him up. 'I belong in this world! It can't be right – it's not justice!'

'You can't stay here,' says Hatch, 'so close to an unguarded portal. You have wronged the people of Orbis and you will face justice there. And don't try to fight it. I've got a whole platoon on the way, just in case there's trouble.'

He doesn't look like he has any fight left in him

though, and Miriam looks almost as battered by it all. She can't look at any of those whom she hurt so badly.

'Here, take these,' I say, holding out my hand to Hatch. Tiny shards of metal and wood; rose-coloured glass and gleaming sprockets. A small pearl from Ursula's comb. All parts of other people's power. 'They were taken from the Anchors . . .'

Hatch carefully wraps them in a handkerchief and tucks them into her pocket.

'Come,' she says to Miriam, and her voice isn't unkind. 'It's time to go.' She snaps cuffs on to Miriam and Lord Rory's wrists, and marches them away. I watch them go, getting smaller, getting further away. The man who stole me. Who dazzled us all, for years, and took so much.

And then I turn back to my parents. There are metres between us, and they're waiting, but I don't know how to cross them.

'Meg,' I whisper, as she nudges into me.

'I've got you,' she says.

'I don't know what to do.'

'You don't have to do anything,' Meg says. 'Just give it a chance – *I'd* give it a chance, if I were in your shoes.'

'You miss your family? Your other family, I mean . . .'

'I do,' she says. 'That never goes away. But then I've got you. I've got Mrs Peters and Great-Aunt Flo – and Iris, too.'

'And Cecil, with his shark stories.'

'They were all true!' he shouts.'

'. . . and none of that is going anywhere,' Meg says.

'Come along, everyone,' Mrs Peters says, shivering. 'Let's go in. Ted can make some tea . . .'

'Oh, Ted can, can he?' Ted mutters.

'Talking about yourself in third person again, Ted!' shouts Meg.

'May we come in too?' asks Callie, arm linked with Frida's, both of them staring with shining eyes as Joe and his father grip each other tightly.

'Of course – all of you,' says Mrs Peters. 'It's not like we have any guests to worry about – Valerie saw them all off with her little magical performance!'

'Do you think they'll come back?' I ask.

'We'll get new guests!' Meg says. 'And now that we've got rid of Rory and all his magic, there'll be no more star storms to put them off. It'll be better than ever.'

'We could have a gym!' says Ted.

Everyone stares at him.

'Well, *I* think it would be a good idea,' he huffs.

'I think there are people from Orbis who would love to visit,' Callie says. 'If you haven't had enough of us all. We can repair the bridge properly, now that the magic is restored.'

Meg claps her hands. 'Now that would be exciting! A guest house full of magicians!'

'A *Ghost House* full of magicians,' says Great-Aunt Flo. 'We're not going anywhere. This is a haunted house – always has been, always will be. Everyone can see that.'

Standing in the porch, listening to the wind howl through the trees, with the pale mist of the river creeping over the grass, it does seem fairly obvious.

I look at my parents and wonder what they think of it all. Of my home. But they don't seem to have noticed the Ghost House – they're just staring at me.

'Inside,' Mrs Peters says, in a gentle voice, and she sweeps us all up and marches us through the lobby.

Chapter 21

We're sitting in the old ballroom that overlooks the viaduct and the thundering waterfall. It's been several hours since we watched Hatch head back over the bridge with Rory and Miriam. Orbis guards met them halfway. Most people have gone to bed, or off to create havoc with the drainpipes.

'Joe, your Anchor,' I say. 'Is it really all fixed now?'

'Pretty much, I think.' Joe holds out his hand. The binoculars perch in his palm, their casing smooth as a new conker.

'How does it feel?' I ask.

'Warm,' he says. 'Like there was a layer missing, and now it's back.'

'Like a cardigan!' trills Meg, perching on the back of one of the old settees.

'I'm glad you're feeling better,' I say.

'You'll feel better still after a little time in Orbis,' says Callie. 'We should head back, Joe. El will be worried, and you need the Orbis air to recover fully. Your father does too . . .'

'I like it here,' says Joe's pa. He stares at the chandeliers and the portraits that hang on the wall over the vast old fireplace. 'But your ma's right, Joe. We need to get back for El. Valerie and her parents have talking to do, and we can come back. The bridge isn't going anywhere this time.'

'Will you be OK?' Joe asks me, as Frida helps his pa up out of his chair. 'I can stay . . .'

'Go,' I say. 'We'll be fine. And I know where you are.'

I watch them go, and then there are no more distractions. Even the drainpipes stop clattering.

Meg frowns. 'I do believe there are spies, trying to listen in,' she says. 'I'll fend them off.' She touches my hand. 'All right?'

I nod. I know it's time. Meg leaves and I turn to them. My parents. They've been so silent. Like ghosts – if ghosts were silent.

*

'You were tiny when you were born,' my mother starts eventually. 'A little bit early, a little bit impatient. But you grew.' She reaches out as if to touch me and then stops herself. 'You were a force of nature. As soon as you could crawl, you were off. And when you found your feet, there was no stopping you.'

'You came everywhere with us,' my father says, smiling. 'We tucked you into your sling and you saw it all. Sunrises in strange lands, roaring seas, mountain trails that led to cities in the sky . . .'

'We had such adventures,' my mother says. 'Orbis has many portals to many different worlds, and we took you to all of them. It was our job to track magic, to discover new places. And we loved it! But . . .' She winces. 'It was foolish of us not to see the danger in it. The theft of that comb left a terrible hole in our world.'

'But it's back now, and we'll heal,' says my father. His beard is more wiry now, and the grey glints in the firelight. 'We need to find ways to use our magic so that we aren't reliant on the Anchors. They make us too vulnerable.'

'There's a way to do that?' I ask.

'There will be,' he says with certainty. I'd forgotten that about him: how reassuring his voice is. 'Now that we have recovered what was lost, Orbis has regained her power. Magic changes, all the time. There has been too much reliance on these . . . things.' He looks at his wrist, at a slim copper bangle that dances with golden flecks.

'They're made in forges,' my mother says. There are shadows under her eyes – she must have been through so much over all these years, but still her dark eyes sparkle. She has a round face, like mine, and hair that clearly misbehaves as much as mine does. 'As soon as a child starts to show their magical ability, they're taken to the Guild. Their Anchor is made in the old forges that melt down old Anchors – everything recycled.'

'We made your pendant in the design of the one your grandmother had, a long time ago,' my father says, as I draw it out of my shirt.

'A little like mine,' my mother says, shifting closer to me and smiling as she shows me hers. Quartz sparks in a copper hoop, hanging from a silver chain. Her smile fades as she looks at me. 'We should have kept you safer. We should have found this place long ago – there was so much magic here. We allowed a complete stranger to use our own magic against us. The last ten years have been indescribable.' She shakes her head. 'We've lost so much time – and here you were, all along.' She shivers, staring out at the river. 'It's very dark here.'

'I'm not afraid of the dark,' I say. 'It's got magic, of its own sort. I didn't remember anything about before. I was just part of this family. My ghost family.'

'And you still are,' my father says. 'That's plain to see.'

'I remember your stories,' I say. 'I didn't think I had memories, but when I saw you both, I could see other things too. I don't know why they hid all this time. I wanted memories, so badly. Now you're here, and I can see a red checked tablecloth, and an egg cup in the shape of a chick . . .'

'Your favourite,' my mother says. 'They will come back, all these memories. Now that we're together again.'

They look up at the ceiling as someone rushes across it, howling at full volume.

'What a home you found here . . .' my father says with a smile.

'Do you want a tour?' I ask.

Their faces brighten, ever the adventurers, and so I show them. The cellar, where Ada and Florence are sitting together on the old chaise longue, the fire bubbling before them. The kitchen, where Ted is prepping for breakfast. We pass Leon, who is taking a booking over the phone – his desk is still in the wrong place – and Mrs Peters' office, where she's busily ordering fresh linen.

Meg joins us, and we head up the stairs, through bright corridors to our attic bedroom. My parents stare like tourists as we go, but they don't look afraid. Their eyes are completely dazzled, just like mine were when I got to Orbis.

Later, we go to the dining room, and Cecil is sitting at the bar. He tells one of his 'big fish' stories, and they listen, entranced, and Mrs Peters tells them that they must stay the night.

'It's not as though we have any other guests to look after,' she says. 'Not yet.'

Then Iris comes and puts on a full show, head backwards and all, and Meg joins her as they whirl through the curtains, and make the silverware tinkle. I sit with my parents in the shifting light of the dancing chandeliers, and for a moment it's like nothing has changed at all, except that my mother's hand is over mine – and my family is *all* here.

Chapter 22

In Orbis, the rivers are golden because that's the colour of the sky. The stars are out night and day, and they're all the colours of a rainbow. They are where our magic comes from.

They reflect in the river, and the whole world is a shining, glittering place. Seven towers stretch from the water up to the sky, all of them pale marble that winks with golden threads.

When we were here last, Ursula's tower stood alone, a shard of darkness that led to stormy skies – but the storm is over. Rory was right when he said that power is never fair. Ursula was one of the most powerful magicians Orbis had ever seen, even though she was so young, and when her comb went missing, the world was rocked for hundreds of years.

Now the forges in the second tower are belching pink smoke. Change is coming. Nobody wants to be parted from their power again so easily. Nobody wants another Lord Rory.

He's in the third tower now. There are silver bars on the windows, and for a moment I think I can see him, his grey hair sweeping up just like it always did, through all the birthdays and the tea parties and the treasure hunts when I was small. I swallow hard, looking away, and Meg winks at me.

'Seeing ghosts?' She sighs. 'I love it here, Valerie.' She stretches, raising her face to the sky. 'It's warm.'

'You're like a cat.' I smile.

'I've never had a cat,' she says. 'Do you think there are cats here? I'm going to investigate . . .'

She spins off into the sky, clearly enjoying the surprise in people's eyes as she goes.

It's been a week. My parents stayed at the Ghost House for three nights before returning to Orbis, and Ted outdid himself with all the poached eggs and jammy cakes, while Mrs Peters tidied the rooms, making way for more guests. A lot of people from Orbis want to visit, now that the bridge is stable again – Hatch and the guards got a whole contingent of Orbis folk to shore it up with their magic when they saw that regular travel would be happening.

'Paying guests!' Mrs Peters kept saying, as she rushed from room to room. 'And no more of those star storms! They all recovered, you know,' she told me yesterday as she flung old pillows out of windows into a skip. 'All the people whose vision was affected. I told them there had been some electrical issues because of the viaduct. There was even a repeat booking!'

'Was it Frankie?' asked Meg.

'It was,' said Mrs Peters with a smile. 'Seems she wasn't put off by your *investigations*. In fact, she's going to bring her famous ghost-hunter friend, and she'll be writing a book while she stays, so you must leave her some time to work!'

'What kind of book?' asked Meg. 'A mystery, with ghosts?'

'Maybe,' said Mrs Peters. 'The important thing is that we have *guests*.'

I grin now, watching Meg spiral over a growing crowd of people before heading over one of the little stone bridges. Joe is waiting on the other side, and for a moment the whole thing seems to swing beneath me, just like the rainbow bridge did that night when we fell into the water.

'You look better,' I say to Joe, when I reach him.

'So do you,' he says. 'Are you ready?'

'Ach, I don't know.' I scuff my feet along the golden pavement. I'm going to the apartment where my parents live. Where *I* lived, for the first couple of years of my life. The memories of it are scant and faded, and I can't help but feel a little apprehensive. 'It won't feel like home, will it?'

'Don't know,' he says. 'I guess it'll be different. Everything's different now.'

'But good?'

'Yes, good,' he says. 'Dad's busy with the Guild forgers, trying to undo our links with our Anchors. It feels really weird after all we went through to get them back, but I'm glad they're doing it. That feeling, when Rory smashed my binoculars –' he shudders – 'like my heart was in a vice.'

We walk to the gleaming courtyard where I first met Callie and the rest of Joe's family, and there they all are, leaning over the balcony. Callie and Frida and El, and my parents, Willa and Fed. All of them gleaming beneath the stardust that falls from the Orbis sky.

My other family.

'We'll come down!' shouts Callie. 'Ursula's waiting . . .'

'It's going to be complicated.' Joe looks up at them all. 'Dividing your time. Can you imagine the birthdays with all these, *and* your ghosts!'

'I reckon we'll manage,' I say with a grin. 'Family's always complicated, isn't it?'

Acknowledgements

My first thanks, in this book written over 2020 and 2021, are to the librarians and the teachers and all the school support staff who have kept the magic of education and reading alive through such difficult times, and to the NHS, the care workers, and all of the key workers – no words will ever be enough.

Specific thanks, then, to the people who have helped to keep the magic alive in me and my writing. To my agent, Amber Caraveo, and to my editorial team Lucy Pearse, Charlie Selvaggi-Castelletti, Gen Herr and Samantha Smith, Rachel Petty and Veronica Lyons, and to the rest of the team at Macmillan Children's Books. Your confidence in me and my work is so shiny, even in spite of all the turbulence – it's a very special gift and I'm grateful beyond words for the last six years. Also, this book was hard and very plotty, and without you all I'd possibly still be lost in the river. A special thanks to Rachel Vale and Helen Crawford-White for another beautiful cover, and to Clare Hall-Craggs and Jo Hardacre, for working through unimaginable circumstances to make sure my books reach their audience.

Finally, very warmest thanks to Aviva Epstein and Caroline Pennington, for going through it all with me; and most especially of all, thank you to Lee, Theia, Aubrey, Sasha, Rocky and Luna. You mean the world to me, and when our world got smaller I was so grateful that we had each other.

About the Author

Amy Wilson has a background in journalism and lives in Bristol with her young family. She is a graduate of the Bath Spa MA in Creative Writing. *A Girl Called Owl* was longlisted for the Branford Boase Award, nominated for the Carnegie Medal and shortlisted for a number of regional awards. Her middle-grade novels include *A Girl Called Owl*, *Owl and the Lost Boy*, *Snowglobe*, *Shadows of Winterspell* and *A Far Away Magic*.

'The rising star of children's fantasy' *Telegraph*

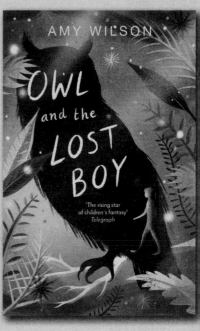

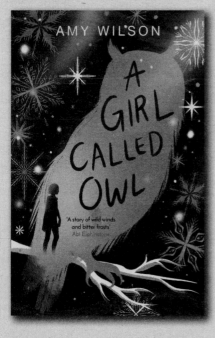

'Beautifully written and totally bewitching'
Sophie Anderson, author of *The House with Chicken Legs*

AMY WILSON

Shadows of Winterspell

Deep in the forest,
magic is waiting

AMY WILSON

A Far Away Magic

Both are lost –
magic will find them

Original and compelling ... an
unexpected tale of grief, magic and monsters
Kiran Millwood Hargrave, author of
The Girl of Ink & Stars

AMY WILSON

Snowglobe

Enter a thousand worlds